Amy Cross is the author of more than 100 horror, paranormal, fantasy and thriller novels.

Days 5 to 8

AMY CROSS

First published by Dark Season Books,
United Kingdom, 2018

First published in April 2013 as part of *Mass Extinction
Event: The Complete First* Series. This edition originally
published in July 2018

ISBN: 9781718001114

Also available in e-book format.

www.amycross.com

CONTENTS

DAYS
5 TO 8

PROLOGUE

Manhattan, one week ago

"YOUR BROTHER'S OVER THERE!" says Sofie, pointing across the park. "Lizzie! Look, your brother's right over there!"

Turning, I see that she's right. My little brother Henry is sitting on the grass with a couple of his friends. My first reaction is that something seems strange about the scene, as if it's somehow impossible that he and I could end up hanging out in the same place. After a moment, however, I realize that this isn't so weird after all. Henry's getting older; he's only a few years younger than me, and it's only natural that I should start seeing him out and about, especially on such a gorgeous summer's day.

"So can I ask you a question?" Sofie continues, nudging my knee as she offers me some more potato chips.

"What?"

"Your brother. Sometimes he seems a bit weird. Is he, like, alright in the head? I don't mean that in a bad way, I just mean that sometimes he has this look in his eyes, like..." Her voice trails off for a moment. "I don't know how to describe it. I'm sounding like a bitch, but do you know what I mean?"

"Um..." I pause, feeling a little confused. "He's not weird in the head," I say eventually. "He's my brother. He's cool. Annoying, but cool".

"Okay," she replies. "That's cool. Sorry. I didn't mean to say anything".

Lost in thought, I eat some more potato chips before looking back over at Henry. He and his friends are standing up, and they start walking across Central Park. At the last moment, Henry glances back at me and we exchange an awkward smile. "He's growing up," I say quietly.

"My brother's a dick," Sofie says. "Like, the other day, I caught him in my room, just going through my stuff like he had a total right to be in there. Does *your* brother ever do that?"

"No," I say, still watching as he disappears into the distance. "No, Henry's kind of cool. He just plays video games and stuff". The problem is, now that Sofia has mentioned her thoughts about Henry, I can't help thinking that maybe she's right; every so often, I catch a glimpse of something in Henry's eyes. Something dark, as if there are undercurrents in his personality that don't show on the surface. Maybe it's just because he's growing up, but I feel like he's changing in loads of different ways. "He's cool," I say again, as much to convince myself as to convince Sofie.

"So are you coming out next Saturday?" Sofie asks. "We were thinking of trying to get into that club near your place. You know, the one with the neon palm tree over the door".

"You want to go *there*?" I ask, shocked. "That looks like the tackiest place in the world. It's a total dive!"

"Exactly," she replies with a grin. "We're thinking they're so desperate for customers, they'll have no problem letting us in, even if one or two of us don't quite have the necessary I.D., if you know what I mean".

"Speak for yourself," I reply. "I'm old enough to go into a bar. I just don't want to". I pause for a moment. "You're old enough too".

"But my little sister isn't," she says. "I really just wanna take her out and show her a good time, especially..." She pauses, and finally she lets out a huge sneeze. "Sorry," she continues, "I just wanna show Naomi a fun evening. You know, so she doesn't get overwhelmed when she's old enough to go out for real. So are you in or are you out?"

"I don't know what I'm gonna be doing," I reply. "A week's a long time".

"But you'll try?"

"I'll try," I say, "but don't hold me to it, okay? The last thing I want to do is go to some ass-crack club and spent the night standing in a corner while dumb-asses dance all over the place".

"It won't be like that," she says, grabbing my arm. "Come on, Lizzie! Lighten up a bit! It's gonna be fun! You, me, Naomi, maybe some other people. We might even meet some guys. You could even invite your brother, but I don't think there's a fake I.D. in the world that'd get him through the door".

"I'll be there if I can," I say. "If it's at all possible, I'll come with you, okay?"

"You'd better," she replies, before sneezing again.

"You okay?" I ask. "You're not coming down with something, are you? You'd better not have dragged me out here just so you can infect me!"

"I'm fine," she says. "I've kind of felt for a while like I might be about to get some massive cold, but it never actually happens. I guess I've just got the most amazing immune system in the world. Probably all the juice I drink".

"Yeah," I reply, rolling my eyes. "That'll be

it".

"So do you wanna come shopping this afternoon?" Sofie asks. "I mean, just window-shopping. I don't have any actual money, but we could take a look around. Unless you've got anything better to do".

"Nope," I reply, "I actually have absolutely *nothing* better to do. Sad, huh?" Sighing, I glance across the park again, but this time my brother is way out of sight. It's weird, but I didn't like the way he kind of ignore me just now. I'd have thought he'd at least come over, but he basically ignored me. I guess he's growing up and he thinks I'm not cool. That's his choice, but I hope he grows out of it soon. I'm already barely speaking to Mom, and Dad's almost never around. The last thing I need is to be on bad terms with another family member. Taking a deep breath, I decide to make an effort to spend a little more time with Henry over the next few weeks. After all, it's not like we have a big family. We need to stick together.

DAY 5

ELIZABETH

Manhattan. Today.

"ELIZABETH!" A VOICE CALLS out in the distance, and I immediately tense up. "Elizabeth! You down here?"

Closing the book, I hurry through to the hallway and double-check that the bolt has been slid across on the door. At least this way, my brother Henry won't be able to get into the apartment, even if he's got Bob's master-key for the whole building. I'm in Harrison Blake's old place, thanks to the key he left behind for me, and I've spent the morning - since sunrise, anyway - reading a book about infectious diseases. So far, Henry and Bob have no idea that this library exists, but it's clear that I'm gonna have to work a little harder to make sure the situation doesn't change. Right now, this apartment is a kind of sanctuary, and it's the place where I come to get away from the others. It's mine, not theirs.

"Elizabeth?" Henry calls out, suddenly sounding much closer. After a moment, the door handle turns and he tries to get in, but the bolt remains in place. There's a pause, followed by the sound of some keys jangling, and finally he tries to unlock the door. Again, the bolt keeps him out. "Assholes," Henry mutters, before starting to walk away. "Elizabeth!" he calls again, getting further away until I hear him go through to the stairwell.

Relaxing, I turn and head back through to the front room. I guess it was dumb of me to think that I could just hide away in here and not be bothered. Given the state of the world right now, it's inevitable that Henry and Bob are gonna start questioning my movements. After all, it's not as if I can just go wandering out the door and go visit friends. Making my way over to the window, I look down at the empty Manhattan street, where a couple of abandoned cars sit next to the sidewalk. This is the fifth day, and it's looking less and less likely that anyone's coming to rescue us. In another two days, we'll be coming up on a week since this disaster struck. Whatever happens, I'm starting to think it's permanent.

Although my plan was to read all morning, I

soon find that my head is elsewhere. Henry's attempt to get into the apartment has left me jumpy and skittish, and I can't relax. Deciding to try a new strategy, I grab the book and head out into the corridor, making sure to lock the door after myself. I head to the stairwell and make my way down to the lobby, figuring I should probably show myself and ensure that Henry and Bob don't start asking too many questions about my whereabouts. As soon as I emerge from the stairwell into the lobby area, I can already hear animated discussions taking place in the little office. Henry and Bob have formed a tight little duo over the past couple of days, and it's no surprise to find them chattering away.

"Well, here she is now!" Bob says with a broad smile as I wander through to join them. "Your brother here was getting all panicky, Elizabeth. Seems he was worried you'd maybe gone outside by yourself, but I told him there's no way you'd be so foolish".

"That's right," I say quietly.

"Where were you?" Henry asks, eying me with suspicion. He's got his rifle slung over his shoulder; I swear, he even sleeps with that thing these days. I never thought an inanimate object could give someone such an immediate boost of confidence, but the rifle has transformed Henry from a lazy teen to a tense, over-confident little soldier.

"I was up on the roof," I reply. "Reading".

"And what's that you've got in your hand?" Bob asks, still smiling as he cranes his stumpy neck to see the book.

"Something about viruses," I say, holding it up for him to see. "I found it in our apartment, so I figured I'd give it a read. I just figured, you never know when it might be useful to know something".

"That's not from our apartment," Henry spits at me.

"Yes it is, dumbass," I reply.

"Where?"

"It was in Mom and Dad's room".

"Where in Mon and Dad's room?"

"In the closet".

"Where in the closet? Mom and Dad didn't keep books in the closet".

"Well they kept *this* one in there," I say, failing to hide my annoyance at his constant stream of questions.

Henry frowns. He clearly doesn't believe me.

"Come on, you two," Bob says, grinning as if he finds us amusing. "Let's not descend into an all-out family squabble here. Henry, your sister's got a right to read a book, okay? Might even come in useful if one of us knows about that kind of thing. And Elizabeth, it'd be courteous if you could perhaps let other people know where you've been, so as to avoid the need for everyone to get worried.

I'm sure you'll understand why we were slightly concerned, especially given recent developments".

"Huh," I say, turning and looking over at the door that leads through to the back of the building. "How's it going with the girl?"

"Not bad," Bob replies. "We're still not at the point where I'm comfortable releasing her, but we're making progress in getting her to trust us. Why, we even managed to find out her name. Mallory".

"Mallory?" I take a deep breath, feeling a growing sense of unease. Ever since Henry and Bob captured that girl, they've been acting strange, as if their conspiratorial relationship has been taken to a whole new level. Bob's convinced that this Mallory girl is a spy sent by some other survivors to find out what supplies we're hoarding, and it's pretty clear that the process of interrogating Mallory is giving both Bob and my brother a real kick. It's tempting to think that they're actually enjoying the whole thing, although I shudder to think that my little brother might actually be involved in something so dark. Ever since Bob gave him the rifle, though, Henry has been a little different. He seems so easily seduced by the semblance of power and responsibility.

"You wanna come and see her?" Bob asks. "Maybe a woman's touch might help".

I pause for a moment. Although I want to go and see if the girl's okay, I can't bring myself to go through and see how she's doing. "It's okay," I say. "Maybe later". Pausing for a moment, I realize that I'm too scared to go and see this Mallory girl. After all, I'm still slightly worried about what Bob and Henry might be doing to her, but I'd rather not confront that particular problem head-on. Not now, at least. I guess I'm a coward.

"Well," Bob says, slowly rising from his chair and wincing a little as his bones creak, "I guess I'm gonna get back in there. I think we're really getting close to the truth. Just need to keep the pressure on, and she's gonna tell us the truth about why she's here. In the meantime, I was hoping you two could go down to that little convenience store on the corner and see if they're got any painkillers. My old hip's playing up". He limps over to the doorway, before turning back to us. "Could you do that for me?"

"Yes, Sir," Henry says, with military seriousness.

"Actually," I say, looking down at the book, "I was planning to -"

"It's fine," Henry says firmly. "I can go alone". As if to prove the point, he takes the rifle from over his shoulder and starts loading it with a couple of cartridges.

"No," I say, "it's okay. I'll come with you". "You don't have to".

"I want to".

"That's the spirit," Bob says, still grinning. "Brother and sister, working together. Just keep an eye out for any sign that we're being watched. I still think there's a danger Mallory was sent to keep an eye on us, and the last thing we need is for some slick bastards to give us the jump. If you two aren't back in an hour, I'm gonna start worrying, okay?" He pauses for a moment. "No detours. No excursions or adventures. Just get down there, find anything that's useful, and then get back. We'll go on a more exhaustive trip later". With that, he turns and limps away to the back of the building, where I guess he"s going to continue with his amateur-hour interrogation of that poor girl.

"You coming, or what?" Henry asks, holding his rifle as if he expects to use it at any moment.

"Sure," I reply, following him through to the lobby.

"Where'd you really get that book?" he asks as we make our way to the front door.

"I told you, Mom and -"

"Bullshit," he says. Pushing the door open, he leads me out onto the sidewalk. It's still so strange to be out here: the ground is covered in a fine white powder from the thick debris cloud that erupted when the plane crashed a few blocks away, while the deserted streets looking completely unnatural. New York's a city that was built to be noisy and fast and full of people; to see it like this is one of the strangest things I can imagine.

"Stay close to me," Henry says, making a big show of looking both ways to see that we're alone. He's like a kid who's been given a gun and told to go and play like a soldier, except the gun is real and I'm pretty sure he's long past the point where he understood that he should be careful. "Come on," he continues after a moment, making his way along the sidewalk.

"Is this really necessary?" I ask, glancing over my shoulder to see the empty street behind us. "There's no-one around".

"You don't know that for sure".

Stopping suddenly, Henry turns to me. "It's so easy for you, isn't it?" he says with a slight sneer. "You can just stand back and make stupid little comments, while the rest of us have to do all the hard work. Like with Mallory. Do you think Bob and I *want* to have her tied up while we find out why she's here? Of course not, but we have to do it, so that we all stay safe". He pauses for a moment, staring straight into my eyes with an expression that seems to border on contempt. "Me and Bob," he continues eventually, "we'd love to stand back and make sarcastic comments while someone else does the nasty work, but we just can't afford to let that happen. We're the ones who have to do the dirty stuff, the hard stuff, the painful stuff. You get to stand back and pretend you're still a nice person.

That's real lucky of you, Elizabeth. I hope you're grateful".

I swallow hard. While I guess Henry has a point, none of that little speech sounded like it came from him directly. In fact, it sounded like something Bob would say.

"See?" Henry continues, turning and walking toward the convenience store.

"See what?" I ask, hurrying after him.

"You haven't got an answer," he replies. "You know I'm right. People like you, with your morals and stuff, need people like us to do the dirty work".

"People like me?" I ask, shocked at how suddenly Henry seems to have developed this very definite, very rigid view of the world. "People like you? Henry, what are you talking about? It's me! It's Elizabeth!" I wait for him to reply, but he just keeps on walking. "Okay," I continue eventually, "let's just cool it. Let's just agree to disagree, and try to get things back to how they were before, yeah? Don't you remember what things used to be like, when we actually *didn't* hate each other?"

"It's like with Mallory," he continues. "You let me and Bob do all the hard work, so you don't have to get your hands dirty".

"What hard work?" I ask, starting to get worried. "You haven't hurt her, have you? You're feeding her and stuff, right?"

"Of course we are," he spits back at me. "We're not monsters. We're just two men, doing what has to be done".

As we reach the convenience store, Henry stops and peers through the broken window. He and Bob have been here before, but there's still plenty of stock left on the shelves.

"What's wrong?" I ask.

"Just making sure we're alone," Henry replies, staring into the gloomy store.

"So we can go back to how things were?" I ask. "At least between us. Right?"

He pauses for a moment. "I didn't like how things were," he says eventually, stepping carefully through the broken window. "Some things are better now".

"Some things are -" I start to say, shocked that he could even think such a thing.

"You need to wait here," he says, interrupting me. "If you see or hear anything, come and find me, okay? This place has two floors, so I might have to go up. The best thing is for you to stand right here and watch out, to make sure no-one comes alone and ambushes us. But if you get the slightest hint of trouble, you need to come and find me".

I stare at him for a moment. "Sure," I say eventually, feeling as if there's no point even trying to reason with him. Somehow, it's as if my little brother has vanished, replaced by this wannabe soldier who gets his orders direct from Bob. Even if the whole world went back to normal tomorrow, I feel as if Henry would never be the same again. Something's changed deep inside his heart.

"I won't be long," he replies, making his way through to the back of the store.

Once I'm alone, I take a deep breath and look up at the dull gray sky. Ever since the power went off, the weather's been kind of like this, especially while the fire from the crashed plane was still burning. This morning, the plume of black smoke seems much thinner, as if the wreckage is finally starting to burn out. In a sick, twisted kind of way, I actually get a little comfort from the thought that at least one of the fires is coming to an end. Sighing, I realize how rapidly my perspective has changed over the past few days. I guess it's inevitable that people grow up when they're thrown into a situation like this. I just wish Henry had a better role model; I wish there was someone around, other than Bob, to show my brother how to be a man.

Lost in thought, I almost don't notice the distant banging sound. Eventually I look across the street, as I realize I can hear a noise far away, almost as if someone is banging on metal. Taking a few steps over to the street corner, I spot a dust-covered red car parked slightly askew about two hundred meters away, and to my surprise I realize there's a hint of movement behind the windshield. Seconds later, there's more movement, and the occupant of the car starts banging furiously on the inside of the windshield. It's almost as if someone's trapped in there, and calling for me to go and help.

THOMAS

Oklahoma

"YOU'RE DRUNK," I SAY, looking down at Joe as he frowns up at me from the ground. With an empty bottle of whiskey just a couple of feet away, it's not exactly hard to see what happened last night. It's not surprising, either: Joe's always taken the easy way out of every situation, and he's doing it again. Right now, he can't even focus on me properly; I guess his world's spinning after another night on the liquor.

"Am I?" he mutters.

"You can't drive like this".

"Sure I can". He tries to get up, but the process is clearly way too difficult; instead, he ends up staring around at the grass, looking a little confused. "Is there a really quiet earthquake?" he asks after a moment.

"I'll drive," I say.

He shakes his head. "Just 'cause I can't walk, don't mean I can't drive". He hiccups. "It's two completely different skill-sets, bonehead. You'll just have to help me to the truck, that's all. Come on, let's get this show on the road". After a few seconds, he curls over onto his side. "I'll wait for you here," he murmurs. "Come and get me when you're ready. I'll just be resting here, ready for the journey".

Without saying anything, I turn and walk away, making my way around the barn until I come to the house. I haven't been back inside since last night, since that final conversation with my mother. Sleeping in the barn, I heard nothing all night except light rainfall on the roof, but now it's morning and I'm faced with the task of checking to see whether my mother survived the night. I'd give anything to not have to go inside and face the truth, but there's no way I can just drive off to Scottsville and leave her here. The worst thing is that, deep down, I think there's a part of me that actually *wants* her to be dead, not only so that her pain is over, but also so that I don't have to be there when she finally passes.

"Mom?" I call out as I step through the front door. The house is eerily quiet, and I feel like I can kind of tell already that she's dead. As long as I can remember, I've never known my mother to be totally quiet: she's always been busy in the kitchen, or busy with the laundry, or she has the radio on, or some other kind of activity. It's almost like she's scared of silence. Right now, however, the house is silence.

Getting no reply, I walk slowly through to the kitchen, and that's when I see her. Sitting at the kitchen table, fully dressed and with a pen in her hand, as if she's writing in her notebook, she's staring at the door, with her eyes wide open. I stare back at her, and for a moment I actually start to think that she might be alive. It's only a few seconds later that I realize there's a glassy, vacant quality to her expression. When I move over to one side of the room, she doesn't acknowledge me at all.

She's dead.

Taking a deep breath, I force myself to stay calm. On the table in front of her, the notebook is covered in blood. I guess she continued to cough her guts up during the night, and eventually she stopped caring enough to wipe it away. Her skin is a kind of yellow-gray color, just like Lydia's when *she* died, and there's a trace of blood in the corner of her mouth. With no idea what I should do, I just stand and stare at her, waiting for something to happen. The kitchen seems so still and so quiet, it almost seems sacrilegious to move to to make even the tiniest noise, but eventually I make my way a little further around the table, and that's when I realize that there's something wrong with her stomach.

She's bloated.

More than bloated, actually: her stomach is distended so much, it almost looks as if she's pregnant. I guess it's the same thing that happened to Lydia, and even the slightest pressure would probably made her explode in the same way. Realizing that there's no way I can risk something like that, I decide that the best thing to do would be just to get what I need, and then get out of here. Hurrying over to the fridge, I grab the last few bottles of water and a few items of food, and then I take some pain-killers and a box of matches from the cupboard. Heading back over to the door, I stop for a moment and look back at my mother one final time. I'd love to see what she was writing in her notebook, but I can't take the risk of disturbing her, so instead I head back outside.

I make my way quickly over to the truck, where I start checking through the provisions we've got stashed, ready for our journey to Scottsville. Although I'm still fighting back tears, I find that keeping busy is a good way to keep from breaking down. Instead of thinking about my mother, I fill my mind with more practical matters about the journey that Joe and I are going to take. I focus on stowing everything securely in the back of the truck and making sure that there's no danger of us losing anything; I fixate on the tiniest details, using all this unnecessary fuss to force other thoughts out of my mind. It works, too, and eventually I realize I've managed to keep myself busy for almost an hour. Finally, pausing for a moment, I lose my focus and all the negative thoughts rush back into my mind. In the space of just a few days, I've lost both my parents, and I've seen a stranger die, and I've seen a plane come down in the woods a few miles away. I swear to God, if I actually sit down and think about all of this, I'm going to go crazy. Better to keep busy, I guess; better to focus on what needs doing.

I turn and look at the house.

We can't just leave her there. We have to bury her. Or something. We have to do something.

Heading back around to the other side of the barn, I find that Joe has managed to go back to sleep. Snoring loudly, he's clearly in that vague zone between being drunk and being hungover; either way, there's no chance of getting any sensible ideas out of him. It's pretty clear that if I wait for Joe to be useful today, I'm gonna be waiting a long time. There's no use even waking him up to tell him about our mother, since he'd probably just forget and I'd have to tell him all over again once he sobered up. Instead of disturbing him, therefore, I head over to his little alcohol stash and, one by one, I open the bottles and pour their contents out onto the ground. It's kind of satisfying, seeing the amber liquid spilling out of the bottles, and thinking about how mad Joe's gonna be when he finds out.

Stopping for a moment, I turn and look over at the house. With a heavy heart, I realize there's still one final job that I need to do before Joe and I leave.

ELIZABETH

Manhattan

"IF THIS IS MORE of your bullshit," Henry says angrily as I lead him out of the convenience store and over to the street corner, "I swear to God, I'm gonna -" He stops speaking as he sees the figure moving around inside the car. To be honest, I'm slightly relieved by his reaction, since I'd started to wonder whether I was going mad. I half-expected Henry to tell me I was imagining the whole thing.

"See?" I reply. "There's someone in there".

"Fuck," he mutters quietly.

"What do we do?" I ask.

"It might be a trap," Henry says, turning and looking back the other way. "It's got to be a trap".

"It's someone who needs help," I point out.

"How do you know that?" Henry asks. "Seriously, you wanna just go walking over there and open that door? How the hell do you know that there's not a bunch of men with guns hiding behind that car? How do you know there's not snipers hiding in windows, waiting to pick us off?"

Sighing, I turn to him. "Because I'm not riddled with paranoia," I reply. "Think about it, Henry. If there were snipers, they could just as easily shoot us now, rather than wait for us to go over there. If there are men with guns, they could just jump us while we're standing here. And anyway, when the hell did you start assuming that everyone's like that? People aren't just gonna turn into a bunch of murderers, just because things changed".

"Hungry people are dangerous," he replies.

"That's exactly what Bob said the other day," I tell him. "Exactly, word for word, those are the words that came out of his mouth. What are you, some kind of parrot?"

He pauses for a moment. "You're right. I'm going over to take a look".

"No," I say, grabbing his arm, "you're not".

Smiling, he turns to me. "I thought you just told me I shouldn't be scared?"

"That's not the same as saying you should go over there!" I reply, suddenly realizing that I might have accidentally filled his mind with bad ideas.

Henry's pretty unstable right now, and the last thing I need is for him to try to prove himself by marching headfirst into a dangerous situation. "We should go and get Bob".

"In a minute," Henry says. "First, we need to understand what we've got here. We're not kids, Elizabeth. We don't have to go running to fetch an adult every time we see something moving".

"No," I say, trying to grab the rifle. "We're *not* going over there".

"Then *you* stay here," he replies firmly, pulling away from me. "Two minutes ago, you were telling me to ignore Bob. You were telling me I'm wrong to let him tell me how to behave. And now, when I want to do something for myself, you insist we go running back to him so he can tell us what we should do. Make your fucking mind up, Elizabeth. You can't be against him when you're confident but then run to him when you're scared".

I open my mouth to argue with him, but suddenly I realize that he might, at least in part, be right. I'm filled with this belief that we should go and get Bob, and that somehow Bob's gonna tell us what to do. In reality, the only thing Bob would probably do would be to grab a rifle and go over to the car. Still, I hate the idea that Henry thinks he can somehow keep us safe simply because he's got a rifle. It's pretty clear that whatever's happening right now, it's not something we understand.

"We'll check to see what's happening," Henry says, trying - and failing - to sound confident, "and then we'll go back to the building and consult with Bob. I'm not saying we should go over there and drag this guy from the car, but at least we should find out what we're dealing with before we go back. We can't just go back to Bob and tell him some vague story about a man in a car".

"It might be dangerous," I point out, feeling disappointed by my reaction. Just a few minutes ago, I was chastising Henry for believing Bob's paranoid ramblings, and now *I'm* the one who's scared. I guess maybe Henry was right when he said that it was easy for me to pontificate about the 'right' thing to do. Suddenly, I have to back up my words with actions, and my heart is racing so fast, I feel as if it's going to explode at any moment. "We have to be careful," I say after a moment.

"If there's any sign of danger," Henry whispers, "we turn and run. You got that? No risks. We turn and run at the first hint that anything's wrong, and..." He pauses for a moment. "If one of us gets left behind, the other one just keeps running".

"I'm not sure about that," I say.

"Stay close to me," he replies.

"Sure," I say, keeping my eye on the car up ahead. It's still hard to make out what's happening inside, since most of the car - like everything else around here - is covered in the same fine blanket of white dust that fell after the power went out. The figure inside is definitely moving, but we're too far away to even tell if it's male or female.

"How many people do you see?" Henry asks as we get to within fifty meters of the car.

"Just one," I reply.

Up ahead, the occupant of the car starts banging harder than ever on the windshield, and waving to catch our attention.

"Think about it," I say to Henry as we edge closer. "Something about this whole situation just doesn't make sense. If this person's been in the car since all of this started, why's he only just started to call for help? We've been outside before, right? If he was banging, we'd have heard him. Why would he wait so long to make a noise?"

"Maybe he was unconscious for a while," Henry replies. "Maybe he was scared. Maybe he only just got here. I don't know, but if you want to go back, I understand. Maybe this kind of thing isn't for you". As if to prove his point, he raises the rifle a little higher.

"I'm not going anywhere," I tell him, even though I desperately want to turn and run. I remember my father telling me once that bravery isn't about the absence of fear, it's about being scared but doing something anyway. If that's the case, then I must be the bravest person in history, since I'm absolutely terrified right now. Still, I can't leave my brother to deal with this alone, because otherwise I'd not only be a hypocrite, but I'd also be pushing him further and further into Bob's embrace.

"It's a guy," Henry says after a moment.

"Are you sure?"

"Yeah. Can't you see? But..." He stops walking and pauses, as if he's hesitant about getting too close. "Something's not right," he continues after a moment.

"What do you mean?" I ask.

"You should wear your glasses more often," he says. "Can't you tell? The way he's moving, it's kind of weird. Jerky. Stiff. There's definitely something wrong with him. Anyway, why doesn't he just get out of the car?"

"Maybe we should go back," I say. My heart's beating so fast right now, I feel like I might faint. Looking up at the windows of the surrounding buildings, I realize I've bought right into the fear and paranoia that I dismissed a couple of minutes ago. I've gone from calling Henry crazy for thinking there might be snipers, to feeling as if someone might start shooting at us while we're talking. It's so weird to realize how quickly my mind can be changed by new developments. This whole thing seems like an unnecessary risk, but at the same time I feel as if we have to find out what's happening.

We've lived in fear and ignorance for almost five days now.

"I'm going closer," Henry says eventually, although I can sense the tension in his voice.

"But if -"

"He's in the car," he replies firmly. "He clearly can't get out. Besides, I've got this". He taps the rifle, before suddenly kneeling down and getting a different view of the car. "There's no-one hiding. You can see if you look underneath. This isn't a trap".

"At the first sign of trouble -" I start to say.

"I know," he says. "Don't worry. I've got two cartridges loaded and ready to go".

As we move closer to the car, I find myself wondering if Henry could really use the rifle. I mean, it's one thing to carry it about and feel like a big man, but it's something else entirely to actually use the damn thing and kill someone. Could Henry actually pull the trigger? After a moment, I realize that the answer is pretty clear. Of course he could. Whatever's changed in him since he became Bob's eager little discipline, it's instilled a sense of calm in his core that gives me absolute confidence in his sense of determination. Basically, I feel safe with him. It's crazy, but even the fact that he has a gun is, in a way, reassuring. I hate guns, but right now I'm so glad that Henry's got a rifle in his hands.

"What the fuck is up with this guy?" Henry

whispers as we get a few meters from the car. "Why can't he just open the door?"

Now that we're closer, I can see what Henry means. The man is staring straight at us, although it's hard to make out his features since there's so much dust everywhere. It's clear, though, that the man's movements are strange, as if he's jerking around slightly as he continues to bang on the window. It also looks like there's something wrong with his hands, as if they're not quite the right shape.

"I'm gonna get a better look," Henry says, stepping over to the car.

"Be careful," I hiss.

"He can't get out," Henry replies, as the man continues to bang on the glass. Reaching out, Henry slowly starts to wipe the dust away from the window, and that's when we both see the man's face. "Holy shit," Henry says, taking a step back. "Holy fucking shit, Elizabeth, what the hell is wrong with this poor fucker?"

Shocked and barely able to even think, I stare at the man and see that his skin seems to be kind of rotten and putrid, as if he's been dead for a few days. His eyes are yellowy-brown and as he places a hand on the glass, it's clear that his body has started to decay. At the same time, he's definitely moving, and his eyes are fixed firmly on us. I swear, it looks as if he died a few days ago and now his body's jerking around of its own accord.

"Is that a zombie?" Henry asks, holding the rifle up as if he's ready to pull the trigger at any moment.

"Don't be stupid," I reply.

"I'm not. It's a genuine question".

"Zombies aren't real".

"Then what the fuck's wrong with him?"

"We need to get out of here," I say, tugging on his sleeve. "Henry, we need to get out of here right now. Whatever's going on, I don't like it". Glancing over my shoulder, I'm suddenly filled with the feeling that more of these people could turn up at any moment.

"He can't get out," Henry replies. "Look, he's trapped. That's the whole thing. He's trapped in there. The door's locked, or he doesn't know how to open it or something".

"I still don't want to be here," I say, still tugging at Henry. "Come on, let's just get out of here. Let's just -"

"I can see you!" the man suddenly calls out from inside the car. His voice sounds harsh and damaged, and there's something bizarre about the way he tilts his head back slightly to get a better view of us. "You need to help me out". He holds up his arms, to show that his hands are missing. "They rotted," he continues. "When I tried to open the door, they just sloshed right off my wrists"

"Did he just -" Henry starts to say.

"I can see you!" the man says again. "I can see you all! You're right there". He stares at us, his eyes wide. "It worked," he says after a moment. "I can see you! It's dark out here in the sun, but I can see you!"

THOMAS

Oklahoma

AS I EXPECTED, there's a plentiful supply of gasoline in the barn, far more than we could ever take with us. My father has a couple of tractors as well as some other harvesting equipment, so he always kept a couple of big barrels full of fuel, along with a load of smaller containers. We could fill the truck's tank ten times over, and although I figure we should take at least one of the barrels with us, there's no way we can lumber ourselves with every drop. That's okay, though, because I know what I'm gonna do with the spare gas. I'm gonna burn the house down, with Lydia and my mother still inside. It's the only way.

With Joe passed out behind the barn, the

whole job is left to me, which is pretty typical. I roll one of the barrels over to the truck and manhandle it into the back, and then I use the smaller containers to fill the tank until it's full. Once that's done, I fetch the other barrel and roll it to the front of the house, and then I find myself standing on the grass and facing the enormity of what I'm about to do. This is *our* house; we've lived here our whole lives, and my family's lived here for hundreds of years. All those men who worked this land, and now I'm the one who's gonna destroy everything. I feel like such a traitor, but I know that there's no other option. It's not as if we can risk moving the bodies.

"This isn't how I wanted it to be," says a familiar voice in my mind, as I step through the front door and start covering the entrance with gasoline. Glancing over at the garden, I imagine my mother standing there and watching as I set about my grisly task.

"What's wrong?" she asks after a moment. "Why aren't you talking to me? Are you mad at me for dying?"

"I just don't wanna seem crazy," I reply, pouring gasoline over the bottom of the stairs.

"It's a little late for that, honey," she says, "and besides, I won't tell a soul".

"I've gotta do this," I say, heading back outside and walking to the kitchen door, where I pour gasoline all over the steps. "You understand that, right?"

"Of course," I imagine her replying. "It's just that when I imagined my funeral, I always thought it'd be a traditional affair with lots of people coming to stand around my grave. Flowers, that sort of thing. Of course, I hoped I might have grandchildren by then, but that was never gonna happen, was it?" She sighs. "Then again, Thomas, you know what I was like. I quite enjoy a little spectacle, so why not go out in style? It's a shame about the farm, though. This building has been in your father's family for so many generations. It's a shame to see all of that come to an end".

"I've got no choice," I reply, stepping briefly into the kitchen and pouring some gasoline close to the table. I take care not to look directly at my mother's dead body.

"How awful," I imagine her saying. "Have you seen my skin? I look so terrible. Thomas, I hope you won't have nightmares about this".

"I'll try," I say, making my way quickly out of the kitchen and back through to the hallway.

"Have you noticed the flies?" I imagine my mother asking.

"Yep," I say, as I spot a few fat flies buzzing their way down from upstairs. I'm pretty sure they've been getting to work on Lydia's body, which is probably a pretty disgusting sight by now. At least one benefit of burning the house is that I won't have to go up there and see the mess for myself. Things have got so bad, I even find myself thinking that maybe I can hear the occasional noise coming from up there, even though I know for a fact that Lydia's been dead for a couple of days now.

"Do you feel sick?" my mother's voice asks after a moment.

"I'm fine," I say, pouring gasoline over the table in the hallway.

"You don't have a cough, do you?"

"No," I say firmly. "I don't know how or why, Mom, but I'm pretty sure I haven't got whatever you've got. Joe too. Somehow we seem to have got away without picking it up. I guess we were just lucky".

"Still," she continues, "don't take that for granted. You need to follow some basic safety precautions. Did you take the antiseptic wipes from the bathroom cabinet?"

Stepping outside, I turn to look back into the house. The whole place stinks of gasoline now, and it'll only take a single match to start the fire. It's tempting to get going immediately, but I feel as if Joe needs to see this, so I reckon I'll wake him up and make him come and watch. Besides, this isn't just a fire to destroy the house; it's also a fire to mark the passing of our mother and to end her body on its way.

"Thomas?" she asks. "Did you hear what I

asked you? Did you take the antiseptic wipes from the bathroom cabinet?"

"No".

"Well, you *must*. They could save your life. Get back in there and fetch them".

"No way".

"Thomas!"

"I'm not going back in there," I say. "No chance. And you can't nag me anymore. You're dead, remember?"

She sighs. "You shouldn't have thrown that alcohol away. You could have used it to clean wounds".

"I don't plan on getting any wounds".

"You know what I mean".

"I had to get rid of it," I say. "Joe would've drunk it otherwise".

"You need to look after your brother," she continues. "He's in pain. He's a troubled boy".

"He's a dick".

"He's your brother". She pauses for a moment. "Never forget that, Thomas. No matter how much you hate him right now, he's still your brother, and he's all you've got in the world right now. He's so troubled. I've never been able to work out what's wrong with him, but he's always had that anguished looks in his eyes, even right back when he was a baby. He's not a bad boy, but he's wayward. I'd give anything to still be here, to look after the pair of you, but I'm afraid it's out of my control. The only thing left is for you and your brother to stick together. You need him, and he needs you".

"Not if I go to California and find Martha".

"The three of you need each other," she says. "Brothers and sisters should stick together. God only knows what she must be going through right now. That poor girl. She was always so self-sufficient, but she must be terrified".

"I wish she was here," I say. "I wish she was right here, and Joe was far away. Martha's way more sensible than Joe. He's a fucking idiot".

"Language, Thomas," my mother's voice says. "I don't want you becoming foul-mouthed. We get enough of that from your brother". She pauses. "I'm serious. If you go around swearing and cursing, it'll reflect badly on me. I want you to promise, right now, that you won't do that sort of thing. As a mark of respect for your father and me. Let this be the last thing you ever promise either of us".

"Okay," I say reluctantly. "But I can't promise it won't ever happen in the heat of the moment, when Joe's really getting at me. Deal?" I wait for her to reply, and then I realize that she's not there anymore. Not that she was there to begin with. It's all just part of my imagination. "I'm going fucking nuts," I say out loud. "Sorry, Mom".

Making my way back over to the barn, I double-check that Joe's still passed out on the grass before I head over to the truck and make final preparations for the journey. I figure we'll need to get out of here soon after we've started the fire, so I want everything to be planned out perfectly. With Joe showing himself to be so completely useless, I feel like I want to prove that I'm the opposite: I can organize things and get things ready, and I can make sure that everything's in order. Pausing for a moment, I try to imagine what would happen to Joe if I just took off right now. There's little doubt that he'd end up dead, and in a kind of cold-hearted way, I can't help wondering if that might be the best thing for everyone. I mean, I'd effectively have twice as long to last on my supplies, and I wouldn't have to worry about Joe arguing with me and trying to get us to do dumb things.

Sighing, I realize I couldn't actually leave him behind. Not yet, anyway. I feel like I have to give him one more chance to prove that he can be useful. I guess, when all things are said and done, he's still my brother, and there's something to be said for that.

Suddenly, realizing I can hear a noise nearby, I turn and look toward the forest. At first, I don't see anything; still, there's a kind of rustling sound, and it definitely seems as if something is moving nearby.

"I can see you!" says a voice suddenly. It's a rasping, grating voice, and I turn around, trying to work out where it comes from. After imagining the voices of my dead parents, it's tempting to think that I've opened the gates of madness and now I can't stop hearing voices, but there's something different this time. This voice is real.

"Hello?" I call out, hurrying around the truck. My heart's racing as I try to work out where the voice is coming from, and finally I spot him. Over in the tall grass, crawling slowly toward me, it's the cop from the other day. The dead cop. His face is all rotten and busted, turned gray-green like my mother's but with pieces missing. He looks like something straight out of a horror film, and his yellow eyes are fixed right on me as he slowly makes his way closer and closer.

"I can see you!" he calls out again. "I can see you all! You're right there". He's only a few meters away now. "It worked," he continues. "I can see you! It's dark out here in the sun, but I can see you! I can see you! I can see all of you. Help me out of here! Help me up! Help me in!". He reaches up toward me, and I step back in order to keep well away from his rotten, discolored hand. "Help me!" he rasps. "I need to rest. Take me into the house".

ELIZABETH

Manhattan

"HE'S TRAPPED IN THERE," Henry says firmly, with the gun aimed directly at the car. "He can't get out. Just focus on that. He can't get to us. He's trapped".

"Uh-huh," I reply, glancing along the street. "And what if he's not alone?"

"We're safe," Henry says, his voice wavering a little. I can tell he's terrified, but I guess he's determined to act like he's in control of the situation. In fact, over the past couple of days, he's started to become more and more like a pint-sized parody of Bob. "It's okay, Elizabeth," he continues. "We need to find out what's happening here".

"I can see you!" the man shouts again,

narrowing his eyes a little. "I can see all of you. Help me out of here! Help me up! Help me in!" He blinks a couple of times. "Help me! I need to rest. Take me into the house".

"He's crazy," Henry whispers to me.

"It's taken me all this time," the man continues. "I've had to learn it all again. I thought it'd be instant, but it's taken me a while to work out how to even do the simple things. How long has it been? Can someone tell me the date? Things look so different". Slowly, he raises his hand again, and he stares at his fingers as if they're the most amazing thing he's ever seen. "This one, anyway," he says. "Each one is slightly strange, but I'm learning. It's so unusual, losing all the little things". He looks back at us. "Why can't I get you all? Why are you still here? You were there when he attacked me".

"Should we say something?" I whisper to Henry.

"Like what?" he hisses back at me. "Seems like he's having his own private conversation". "I heard that!" the man shouts. "Why can't I hear you? This is so much different to how I planned. I should have known. I suppose I was arrogant, but that's in the past. I don't remember anything after the airport. What was her name? Where am I? Not me. What did you say? Where's the real me? Where's the first one? They all look the same". He pauses for a moment. "Help me," he says eventually. "I think I need to find the original".

"I don't know what he's talking about," Henry whispers to me. "It's not making any sense".

"He mentioned the airport," I reply, suddenly filled with the idea that maybe this guy, even in such a terrible state, might be able to tell us what happened out there. The airport is where our parents were, back when this whole thing started, and I've been clinging on to this increasingly desperate hope that perhaps they might have survived. Stepping forward, but making sure I don't get too close, I stare straight into the man's eyes for a moment. "What happened at the airport?" I ask, shaking so hard, my teeth are almost chattering. "Did you see what happened out there?"

"It was bad everywhere," he replies, his yellowy eyes staring at me. "I knew it'd be bad, but it was worse than I could ever have imagined. Or better. One of the two, anyway". He pauses. "I'm not talking to *you*". "Did people get away from the airport?" I ask. "Did people survive? Are they coming this way? Is that where you came from? The airport?"

"Who's Joe? Which airport? There are so many. The world's filled with airports, you know".

"Let's get out of here," Henry says, grabbing my arm. "Elizabeth, we need to get moving. We need to get Bob. He'll know what to do".

"Who's Bob?" the man asks, frowning.

"This guy might know about our parents," I say to Henry, pulling away from his grip.

"Elizabeth!" he hisses. "Look at him! He doesn't even know where he is! It's like his brain's totally garbled".

"I'm not sorry about your mother," the man says suddenly. "Even if you burn it, you won't achieve anything. Burn the whole planet, you still won't get it all. You can't teach poor old Joseph about these things. You can't even begin to..." His voice trails off.

"What about my mother?" I ask. "Tell me about her".

"You have no idea how long it took me to get here," he continues. "I had to drag myself through the bushes. I was so slow, and I was distracted by so many things. It's not easy, using all these things at once. Even after everything that happened, there are so many to deal with. It's so much harder than I guessed. I got so many things right, and so many things wrong. It's taken me so long to understand my limitations, but it doesn't really matter. I'm working through it. That's one of the best parts of the whole thing, really. I can continue to learn as I go along. I can work out more and more". He pauses. "Of course it doesn't make sense to you. You're an idiot. If it made sense to morons like you, the world would never have got into this mess in the first place".

"You mentioned my mother," I say firmly, feeling as if I might cry at any moment. "Did you see her? What happened to her?"

"Elizabeth!" Henry hisses. "He doesn't even *know* Mom and Dad. You can't trust anything he says, he's lost his mind. Come on! We need to go and get Bob!"

"What happened at the airport?" I ask, inching closer to the man in the car. "Tell me what happened at the airport".

"Probably the same as everywhere," the man replies, looking down at the car door. "I can do this," he says after a moment. "I can definitely do this. I could do it before. It's just going to take a little time. This grass is so cold and damp. Help me into the house". He seems to be fiddling with something in the car, and suddenly there's a clicking sound.

"Get back!" Henry shouts, pulling me away from the vehicle as the door swings all the way open and the man hangs out, still held back by his safety buckle.

"I have to learn everything again," the man says. "Even that stupid car door took me so long. Why can't I get out now? Is there something? I forgot about timezones. Can you believe I was so stupid? It never occurred to me that it might be the middle of the day in New York but the middle of the night in Tokyo. Day and night at the same time". He pauses for a moment, and then suddenly, with no warning at all, he lets out a loud and terrifying scream, as if he's in agony.

"Fuck this," Henry says, raising the barrel of the rifle.

"What are you doing?" I ask him.

"Putting this son of a bitch out of his misery," he replies, aiming carefully as the man continues to scream as loud as possible.

"You can't *kill* him!" I shout, pushing the gun away just as he pulls the trigger. The shot echoes between the tall buildings, and a piece of masonry explodes in a shower of dust.

"Fuck you!" Henry shouts, pushing me back. Losing my balance, I topple down to the ground. Before I can get back up, Henry aims once again and fires. This time, he's right on target: I look over at the car just in time to see the man's upper chest explode in a shower of blood; he jolts for a moment, and his arm twitches a couple of times before he falls completely still.

"Come on," Henry says, grabbing my arm as I stand up. "We're going back!"

"Why did you do that?" I ask, watching as blood and pus flows out of the man's chest and down onto the tarmac. "What the hell's wrong with you?"

"Let's just go," Henry says, pulling me along

the street. "We can talk about it later".

"You didn't have to do that," I say. "He wasn't come at us. He was just talking".

"He was fucked," Henry replies firmly. "You heard him. He was talking crap".

"So you shot him?"

"I had to make a decision".

"Are you okay?" I ask as we reach the corner and make straight for our building. "Henry, seriously, is something wrong?" When he doesn't reply, I decide to just wait a few minutes. I don't care how tough he acts, he has to be affected by the fact that he killed that man. There's also the question of the man himself, and the things he said. Even though he was talking, he looked dead. I don't believe in ghosts and zombies and things like that, but I know enough to trust my own eyes. As we reach the building and head into the lobby, I can't help glancing back the way we came, just in case there are more of those things outside. Suddenly, this city feels like a far more dangerous place.

THOMAS

Oklahoma

AS THE DEAD COP continues to crawl toward me, I keep stepping back. There's a part of me that wants to run, but at the same time I'm almost mesmerized by his appearance. With his discolored skin and his yellow eyes, he bears more than a passing resemblance to my mother, and to Lydia, after they were killed by the virus, and it looks as if there's blood all over his shirt. It's almost as if he burst but somehow managed to stay alive. Still, he's moving so slowly, I'm pretty sure I can keep away from him without too much trouble. It's not like he can suddenly leap out and surprise me.

"You need to help me out," he continues, his voice sounding so old and tattered, as if the process of decay has spread all the way down his throat. "They rotted. When I tried to open the door, they just sloshed right off my wrists. It's taken me all this time. I've had to learn it all again. I thought it'd be instant, but it's taken me a while to work out how to even do the simple things. How long has it been? Can someone tell me the date? Things look so different".

"What do you want?" I ask, still edging away from him. As he crawls closer, I can see patches of bone poking through from beneath his skin.

"This one, anyway," he says, frowning at me. Whatever he's talking about, it's as if he's not really reacting to anything I'm saying. "Each one is slightly strange, but I'm learning. It's so unusual, losing all the little things". He looks at me for a moment, as if he finds me to be the most fascinating and confusing thing he's ever seen. "Why can't I get you all? Why are you still here? You were there when he attacked me".

"That was him, not me," I say. "Joe attacked you. I didn't have anything to do with it. I told him not to do it. I thought he was just gonna shoot you!"

"I heard that!" the man shouts suddenly. "Why can't I hear you? This is so much different to how I planned. I should have known. I suppose I was arrogant, but that's in the past. I don't remember anything after the airport. What was her name? Where am I? Not me. What did you say? Where's the real me? Where's the first one? They all look the same".

"What the hell are you talking about?" I ask. "You're not making any sense. Where did you come from? Can you even hear me?" Still fighting the urge to run, I find it hard to believe that this guy is still alive. I can't help thinking that maybe his brain is technically dead, but somehow it's firing off impulses that are driving his body forward. Frankly, that's the only explanation that makes sense: this is some kind of freak reaction, like a malfunction of a human body that has already died.

"Help me," he says after a moment, almost sounding as if he's pleading with me. "I think I need to find the original".

"What?" I reply. "Did you come here for help? We can't help you! There's nothing we can do for you!" Turning to look over at the barn, I realize I need my brother to see this. "Joe!" I shout, trying not to sound too panicked.

"It was bad everywhere," he hisses. "I knew it'd be bad, but it was worse than I could ever have imagined. Or better. One of the two, anyway".

"What the hell are you on about?" I say, moving away as he crawls a little closer to me.

"I'm not talking to *you*," he says.

"Joe!" I shout, looking over toward the barn again. "Joe! Wake up!" "Who's Joe? Which airport?" the cop asks suddenly.

"There are so many. The world's filled with airports, you know".

"I didn't say anything about any goddamn airport," I spit back at him. "There's no airport around here".

"Who's Bob?" the man asks, frowning.

"There's no Bob," I say. "You're fucking losing your mind". It's pretty clear that the cop's brain is totally addled, probably after crawling through the grass for days on end. I wouldn't even be surprised if he's got maggots and stuff crawling through his body. Grabbing one of the cans of gasoline, I remove the cap and throw some over the cop's body. He doesn't seem to react at all, so I carefully move around him and tip the rest of the can over him. Joe was supposed to finish this guy off the other day, but now I'm going to make sure that his suffering is over.

"I'm not sorry about your mother," he says suddenly, as if he doesn't care what I'm doing.

"I'm gonna burn you and I'm gonna burn this house," I say, starting to panic. "I know it's gonna hurt at first, but trust me, it's better than leaving you here. Something's wrong with you, but hopefully you can't even feel pain, okay?" Taking a deep breath, I look up at the darkening sky. "Dear Lord," I mutter, "please forgive me for what I'm about to do. I'm only trying to save him from more pain".

"Even if you burn it, you won't achieve

anything," the cop replies. "Burn the whole planet, you still won't get it all. You can't teach poor old Joseph about these things. You can't even begin to..." His voice trails off. "You have no idea how long it took me to get here," he continues eventually. "I had to drag myself through the bushes. I was so slow, and I was distracted by so many things. It's not easy, using all these things at once. Even after everything that happened, there are so many to deal with. It's so much harder than I guessed. I got so many things right, and so many things wrong. It's taken me so long to understand my limitations, but it doesn't really matter. I'm working through it. That's one of the best parts of the whole thing, really. I can continue to learn as I go along. I can work out more and more". He pauses. "Of course it doesn't make sense to you. You're an idiot. If it made sense to morons like you, the world would never have got into this mess in the first place".

"You're sick," I say. "I don't know if you can understand me, I don't know if you can even hear me, but I'm gonna try to explain it to you real careful and real slow, okay? You're sick. You're really, properly sick, and you're gonna die. I don't know why you're not dead already, but you're gonna die a slow and painful death. I'm gonna save you from that. This is for the best. I'm not murdering you, I'm helping you".

"Probably the same as everywhere," he replies, almost as if he's having some other conversation in his head. "I can do this. I can definitely do this. I could do it before. It's just going to take a little time. This grass is so cold and damp. Help me into the house. I have to learn everything again. Even that stupid car door took me so long. Why can't I get out now? Is there something? I forgot about timezones. Can you believe I was so stupid? It never occurred to me that it might be the middle of the day in New York but the middle of the night in Tokyo. Day and night at the same time".

"Please don't hate me," I mutter. Fumbling for the box of matches in my pocket, I take a deep breath, realizing I'm gonna have to just burn him. We're far enough from the truck now, so it shouldn't be dangerous. Striking the match, I watch the flame for a few seconds before looking down at the cop. He's a few feet from me still, so I figure this is the perfect moment. I have no idea why he wants to reach me, but there's no way I'm gonna let him touch me, and I don't think he's gonna stop until I do this. It's for the best. I'm saving him from the agony of his condition.

"I'm sorry," I say weakly, staring at him, "but this is the only thing I can do to help you".

Without wasting another second, I throw the match at him. Instantly, his entire body goes up in flames, and he lets out a brief scream before falling silent. I stand back, watching in shocked awe as he seems to briefly roll onto his side before he twitches a little and then becomes completely still. For a fraction of a second, I think I can maybe hear him still screaming, but I can't be certain. What matters, though, is that after I've stood and watched the flames for a couple of minutes, I realize he's definitely dead.

As the fire continues to rage, I can see the faintest outline of one of his hands, reaching out from the inferno but remaining completely still as the flames start spreading to the surrounding grass.

ELIZABETH

Manhattan

"WE'RE GOING TO HAVE a new system," Bob says as he flips the steaks on his little portable stove. "We can't afford to have this place unguarded, not even for a second, not now we know for a fact that there are possible threats out there. I want the lobby door locked at all times, and I want someone sitting with a rifle, facing that door, every single hour of the day and night. If anyone tries to get in, we meet them with maximum, lethal force". He slides a steak onto Henry's plate, then one onto mine, and finally a third onto his own. "Until we know definitively what's happening, I'm not taking any chances. The security of this building and its citizens is the most important thing, and I won't allow us to be compromised by anyone or anything".

"I'm sorry I killed it," Henry says, staring down at his food.

"Don't be sorry, boy," Bob replies. "You did what you had to do at the time. I don't deny that it would've been useful to have had one of those things alive, so we could study it, but let's look on the bright side. Hopefully it was a one-off, just an aberration. We might never see anything like it again, but if we do, we'll try to keep it alive so we can find out what it is. For now, though, let's take comfort from the fact that it seemed pretty dumb. I mean, it couldn't even get out of the car, right?"

Looking down at my food, I try to take stock of the day's events. When Bob came back with us to see the dead man in the car earlier, I could immediately tell that he had no idea what he was seeing. Ever since then, he's been trying to maintain the illusion that he's in control, but something seems to have subtly changed. The certain that was such an infuriating part of Bob's character seems to have slipped a little, although over the past couple of hours he seems to have become a little steadier. Still, nothing changes the fact that none of us has any idea what's happening. We're lost and blind in a world that seems to keep throwing surprise after surprise at us, and I can't shake the feeling that despite Bob's bravado, we're slowly sinking.

"There'll be more," I say quietly, suddenly experiencing a moment of total clarity.

"You don't know that," Henry replies.

"It makes sense," I continue. "Why would one of those things exist, but not others? Didn't you see how it was moving when it was talking to us? It was alive, at least partially. It was something else, something different, and there's no way that'd happen just once. There'll be more, I guarantee it".

"You might be right," Bob says, cutting a piece from his steak. "See, Henry? Sometimes you need to listen to your sister". He turns to me. "We're gonna have to train you up on how to use a gun, Elizabeth. Not only for your safety, but for ours as well".

"I don't know about that," I reply. "I don't really like guns".

"A gun ain't nothing to be scared of," Bob says. "Treat it as a tool, treat it with respect, and you've got nothing to fear". "This is a big mistake," Henry says through gritted teeth. It's almost as if he's close to tears.

"Would you rather your sister sat down here undefended?" Bob asks. For the first time, he seems slightly annoyed at Henry, as if he's getting tired of my little brother's tantrums. "What would you have her do? Sit around with a carving knife? Sit down here totally undefended, without even so much as a telephone so she can raise the alarm?"

"You don't know her," Henry says, staring at me. "She's my sister. I know what she's like. She's dumb".

"Thank you," I say, smiling at him.

"You see?" he continues. "She can't even take this seriously".

"Let's just calm down," Bob says. "We need to conserve energy, and you two squabbling is just a nightmare that I don't need right now. We need to work together, not pick each other apart. Henry, your input is appreciated as ever, and I hope you know by now that I value your opinion. However, we need to adapt to the situation, and if that means pulling in more resources, then so be it".

"But if she -"

"That's an order, soldier," Bob says firmly, glaring at my brother with an expression that leaves absolutely no doubt of his seriousness. Once again, Bob seems to be enjoying his role in charge, and now, for the first time, he's having to exercise his full authority and make Henry behave.

"Fine," Henry mutters quietly, though it's clear that he's not convinced.

"What's that, boy?" Bob asks, staring at him.

"Yes, Sir," Henry says, taking a deep breath. "I shouldn't have questioned you. I know you know what you're doing, it's just that sometimes..." He looks over at me, and I swear there's genuine hatred in his eyes. I can't help wondering what, exactly,

Bob has unleashed in my brother. "I'm sure she'll be fine," he says after a moment.

"We'll do some practice work with a gun later," Bob says, turning to me, "just so you can get a basic understanding of how they work".

"I can show her," Henry says darkly.

"No, I'll do it," Bob replies, as if he's intentionally trying to embarrass Henry and push him away. It's pretty clear that Bob likes playing games, and that for some reason he's decided, after a few days of winding Henry closer and closer, to push him away. It seems kind of crazy that, even as we're dealing with a completely changed world, Bob is apparently keen to play mind games; even crazier is the realization that less than a week ago, when everything was normal, I'd barely even noticed that Bob existed, while Henry was just my annoying younger brother who spent too long playing video games. Has it really taken just five days for the world to turn on its head?

The rest of the meal passes in relative silence. There's palpable tension in the air between Henry and Bob, and it's clear that Bob seems to be doing this deliberately. I feel as if I'm being used as a pawn in some kind of private feud between the pair of them, and I want to reach out and help my brother. Unfortunately, I'm pretty certain that Henry would rebuff any attempt at mending the fences between us, so I figure I just need to keep my head down and wait for him to come to me instead. It has to happen eventually.

"I'll do the first night shift," Bob says eventually, as he finishes his steak. "I'll start tonight at 10pm, and then one of you can relieve me at 6am. You can sort it out between you, just as long as one of you'd there to take over. Henry, I'd appreciate it if you could check the roof of the building and make sure there are no unsecured doors or windows up there. I'm starting to think we need to be prepared for attacks from all levels. Elizabeth, we'll meet down here in half an hour and do some work on the guns. There's not much you need to know, but like I said, a little respect and learning goes a long way".

Without replying, Henry stands up, grabs his rifle and walks through to the stairwell. It's pretty clear that he's sulking, and that he hates the fact that Bob seems to be drawing me closer to his 'inner circle'. There's a part of me that's glad to see Henry taken down a peg or two, but at the same time I hate seeing my brother having such a hard time.

"Elizabeth," Bob says after a moment, "I think we need to talk about Henry". Letting out a sigh, he grabs a half-empty bottle of whiskey and pours himself a glass. "Can I offer you a drink?"

I shake my head.

"Suit yourself. More for me". After taking a sip, he sighs again. "I made a mistake. I thought your brother was made of the right stuff, Elizabeth. I thought he could take orders, and I thought he could keep a cool head. Instead, he seems to have this untamed wild streak that just won't be brought under control. I hoped to get his head into the right shape, but it's becoming clearer all the time that it's just not gonna happen. To be honest, I'm starting to worry that I've maybe created a monster".

"He's not a monster," I say.

Shrugging, Bob gets to his feet and heads over to the door. "I'm gonna grab some water," he says, "and then we'll see about your training". With that, he walks away, and I hear his tired feet slugging up the stairwell.

Sitting alone, feeling the weight of the gun in my hand, I try to imagine myself firing it at something. At someone. In my mind's eye, I keep replaying the moment when Henry shot the man in the car, and I try to work out whether I'd ever be able to pull the trigger in such a situation. The truth is, I feel like I could; if my life was in danger, or if the lives of other people were in danger, I feel I could do it. Maybe that makes me a cold-hearted bitch, and it's certainly not something I'd ever have predicted just a few days ago. At the same time, the rules of the world have changed dramatically. If it came down to a kill-or-be-killed situation, I think I could kill. In fact, I *know* I could kill.

I'm terrified of dying.

Looking up, I suddenly realize that I heard a noise in the distance. The hairs on the back of my neck immediately stand up as I imagine a group of intruders breaking through the door at the rear of the building. Sliding the safety switch off, I take the gun over to the door that leads through to the rear of the building. For a moment, there's nothing but silence, but then I hear the noise again: a kind of slipping, shuffling sound. Just as I'm about to turn and fetch Bob and Henry, I hear the noise again, but this time it seems to be a little clearer, and a little more distinct.

Someone's weeping.

It takes a moment before I realize that this must be Mallory, the girl Bob has been keeping tied up. In all the confusion that's occurred today, I completely forgot all about her.

The weeping continues. She sounds truly miserable, as if she's lost all hope.

Glancing over toward the lobby, I see that there's no sign of Bob. I guess he's still on his way up to his apartment. Figuring that I have the gun, so I have no reason to be scared, I force myself to ignore my fears; instead, I make my way through to the next room, and then through to the storage room where Bob and Henry have been keeping Mallory tied to a chair.

"Hello?" I say as I finally spot Mallory at the far end of the dark and gloomy room. She's still tied to the chair, and I can see that there's no-one else around.

The weeping stops.

"I heard you crying," I say, making sure to stay far enough away, just in case she tries something.

"Who are you?" she asks, with her back to me.

"That doesn't matter," I say. "Do you want something? Are you hungry? Thirsty?"

"You have to help me," she says, her voice trembling and weak. "Untie me, before he comes back. He's going to kill me!"

"He just needs to make sure you're on our side," I say, taking a deep breath. My heart is pounding, and I'm convinced that she's going to suddenly burst free from the ropes and make a run at me.

"He's going to kill me," she replies.

"No," I say. "He's just checking that you're -"

"Look at me!" she says, turning so that I can see one side of her face. It's immediately clear that she's got several cuts and bruises around her eyes and cheek. I'm certain that she did have any marks on her when she first came here yesterday.

"How did that happen?" I ask, starting to get a horrible feeling of apprehension in the pit of my stomach. Glancing over at the little wooden table by the wall, I see an array of tools laid out: a hammer, some pliers, some wire, some needles, all of them covered in blood.

"I can't take the pain," she whimpers. "He knows I'm not a threat. He just wants to hurt me".

Stepping a little closer, I keep the gun raised, just in case this is a trap. Still, as I move slowly around the chair, I can see that Mallory's in a terrible state. Her clothes are torn, ripped open in place to expose her naked body. Her face is bruised and battered, and her hands and arms are covered in blood. When I look at her eyes, I see that she's struggling to remain conscious.

"Please," she whispers, with tears streaming down her face, "if you won't let me go, then just shoot me. Do *something*. Before he comes back. I can't take it anymore. Save me or kill me, it's up to you. Just don't let him come near me again. I can't take this anymore. Kill me".

THOMAS

Oklahoma

"WHAT ARE YOU WAITING FOR?" Joe asks, as we stand on the lawn. "You gonna do it, or what?"

We're ready to torch the house, but I can't quite bring myself to strike the match. Not yet. The thought of our family home going up in smoke is bad enough; the thought of our mother's body sitting at the kitchen table, her dried blood on the notebook, a pen in her hand, her eyes staring straight ahead, is just too much to comprehend. I can't keep myself from imagining the flames as they roar through the kitchen, consuming her body, burning her skin to a crisp and eventually leaving nothing but bones. It's such a horrible thought, but I can't stop going over and over and over the same images in my mind, and each time I think of her suddenly looking over at me and screaming as the skin melts from her face.

"You want me to do it?" Joe asks, sounding bored. Since he woke up a few hours ago, hungover and in a foul mood, he's been stomping around like an asshole. He took the news of our mother's death in his stride, saying it wasn't much of a surprise, and he didn't even seem that surprised when I told him about the cop. I guess he doesn't really believe me; he thinks I'm a stupid kid who makes things up and gets hysterical. Even when I showed him the burnt skeleton on the lawn, he just shrugged and acted like it was nothing important. Sometimes, I feel like Joe exists in his own little world where the actions of other people don't matter at all.

"I'm *gonna* do it," I say after a moment. "I just think maybe we should say something first. Like, something as a mark of respect".

"You're gonna torch the place, and you're talking about respect?"

"There's two bodies in there," I remind him.

He shrugs. "You wanna say something, then say something. Otherwise, let's get going. We've wasted today already; I don't wanna waste tomorrow as well. We've gotta hit the ground running".

"If you hadn't been wasted -"

"Get on with it," he says firmly, scratching

his scalp as if he's bored and restless.

Sighing, I stare at the house. "Dear Lord," I say, struggling to think of the right thing to say. I should have listened better, all those times I heard religious people saying important stuff. "Dear Lord, please watch over our mother's soul and... let her into Heaven. She lived a good life, she didn't ever do anything wrong to anyone and she deserves to be up in Heaven now. So does our father, so please let them be together. And Lydia too". I pause for a moment. "Joe, what was Lydia's second name?"

He shrugs.

"Please take Lydia into Heaven too," I continue, "and forgive them all any sins they might have made. Please show your mercy and do the right thing by them all. And please bless our journey, because we're not sure what's going to happen when we get to Scottsville. We pray that you see to it that things get put back to how they were. We pray that not too many people have died. We also ask you to take into Heaven the police officer who -"

"Okay, that's enough," Joe says, grabbing the matchbox from me and striking one of the matches, before holding it out above the trail of gasoline that leads to the house. "It's a shame," he says after a moment, "but I guess it's come to this. Don't thank God. If he's real, this is all his fault anyway". With that, he drops the match. Almost immediately, a line of fire bursts toward the house, up the steps, and in through the front door. For a few seconds, it seems like that's about all that's going to happen, but finally I spot some flames around the back as well.

It's weird, but I assumed we'd just turn and walk away when the fire started. Instead, without saying anything to each other, we just kind of stand there and watch as the fire spreads through the house. After a while, I see an orange glow coming from the kitchen, which means the flames have reached our mother. I try to stop thinking about her body, burning up in the inferno, but I guess it's natural to think about that kind of thing at a time like this. Closing my eyes, I dip my head and say a private little prayer, reminding God that he really ought to let my parents into Heaven, and asking him to show some mercy to those of us who are left down here. I can't help feeling that if Joe and I are going to get through this and work out what's going on in the world, we need to have a little help from a higher power.

"You ready?" Joe says, turning and walking away. "You can drive," he calls back to me after a moment.

Opening my eyes, I feel the heat of the blaze on my face and I realize that although I could stand here all evening and all night watching the fire, it's better if we get moving. Reluctantly, I turn and follow Joe over to the truck. Just as I'm about to get into the driver's seat, I hear a huge crashing sound; looking over at the house, I watch as the entire roof gives way, smashing down and bursting through one of the main walls. Seconds later, another wall gives way and collapses into the flames. Finally, the shape of the house isn't really visible within the fire; it's just a huge blaze, with pieces of wood sticking out from a couple of spots, but you'd never know it was ever a house unless you'd seen it before.

"It's gone," I say quietly, holding back the tears that are welling up behind my eyes. "Rest in peace, Mom".

"I'm gonna sleep while you drive," Joe says, getting into the truck. "My head's fucking killing me".

Once I've got into the driver's seat and started the engine, I switch the headlights on so I can see my way in the late evening gloom, and finally I ease the vehicle down the driveway and onto the main road. Glancing in the mirror, I take one final look at the house, and just for a moment I think I see a figure walking through the flames. It's just my imagination, though, so I accelerate and start us off on the long, dark journey to Scottsville. Within a few minutes, Joe has already started snoring next to me, but I don't really mind. I'm just focused on the road ahead, which is picked out by the headlights, After a while, with no other traffic around, I start to settle into the rhythm of the journey. I reach up and test the radio, but of course there's no-one broadcasting and the dial goes from one end of the spectrum to the other without picking up a signal. Taking a deep breath, I decide to relax as much as I can during the journey itself. After all, we've got no idea what to expect when we reach Scottsville in the morning.

DAY 6

ELIZABETH

Manhattan

THE CITY LOOKS SO strange at night, with no lights and no movement. Skyscrapers rise up like huge monoliths, their dark faces seeming almost like the bare bones of a city that that has had all the meat stripped away. Meanwhile, in a mocking kind of way, the stars above have never seemed brighter. The silence of the city makes everything seem even more bare and desolate, and works as a constant reminder of the noise that has been lost. Standing alone at the broken window in our apartment, I close my eyes and feel the breeze as it brushes past me. It's as if I've been transported to some completely different place, to some other land based on fractured images that come from half-remembered dreams. I can't help wondering whether that old world, my old life, was real.

Hearing a noise in the distance, I open my eyes. Given that there are only four people living in this entire high-rise, any noise is worthy of note. Bob's supposed to be downstairs, keeping guard in case any interlopers turn up at the front door, while my brother Henry is asleep and snoring in his bedroom. The only person left, apart from me, is Mrs. DeWitt, but she hasn't been out of her apartment for a few days. Bob claims to have spoken to her yesterday, and reports that she has some supplies stored away, but I figure she has to come out eventually. Still, it's hard to understand why anyone would be wandering around the building in the early hours of the morning. Try as I might, I can't help being a little worried.

Then again, there's a fifth person. Or at least, there's *supposed* to be a fifth person. Down in one of the rooms at the back of the building, tied to a chair and awaiting her next round of 'interrogation', Mallory is supposed to be fully restrained. That's the idea, anyway. That's the theory. The truth is a little more complicated. Mallory isn't tied to chair. Not now. I let her go a couple of hours ago, but I didn't tell anyone. I'm just waiting for Bob or Henry to realize what's happened, at which point I guess they're raise hell and start trying to track her down. Maybe that's what the noise is, then; maybe it's Bob, racing along the corridors as he tries to find his former prisoner. If that's the case, there's only one thing left for me to do: I have to hope and pray that he won't find out that I was the one who loosened Mallory's ropes and helped her get away.

As I head over to the front door, I remind myself that there's no way anyone or anything could have got past Bob. If he'd fired his rifle down in the lobby, I'm sure I would have heard it, even all the way up here. The odds of the building having been invaded are pretty low, so the most likely thing *is* that Bob has discovered Mallory's absence. Standing by the door, I hear footsteps in the stairwell. Someone's coming up toward this level. I close my eyes again, realizing that I must have been right the first time: Bob has clearly been through to the back room, and he's clearly discovered that Mallory's missing, in which case -

Suddenly there's a loud banging sound on the other side of the door. Taking a deep breath, I force myself to wait a moment, figuring I need to make it seems as if I was asleep. After a few seconds, I open the door and stare at Bob, who has a fierce look in his eyes.

"She's gone!" he says firmly. He clearly assumes that I'll know what he means.

"Who?" I ask.

He stares at me. Out of breath from running up the stairs, he seems kind of wild, almost as if the mask of control has finally slipped.

"The girl?" I ask, surprised at how easy I'm finding it to lie to him. "Mallory?"

"She's *gone*," he says again, pushing past me and entering the apartment just as a sleepy Henry comes through from his room. "The ropes are untied and the back door's open!"

"What do you mean?" Henry asks as he reaches us. "You said -"

Without warning, Bob lashes out and pushes Henry back against the wall. It's a shocking moment of unrestrained anger, and he stares at Henry with an expression of pure rage. "I told you to make sure all the doors were locked," he says. "I told you to make sure there was no way in or out of the building".

"I did," Henry stammers, looking totally confused.

"Then how the fuck did she get out?" Bob asks.

"How did she get out of the ropes?" I say, hoping to distract attention away from the unlocked door in the back of the building. The truth is, Henry *did* lock all the doors, but I managed to briefly lift the key from the desk and open a door in the delivery room while no-one was looking. The last thing I need is for Bob to get angry at Henry for something that was my fault; at the same time, there's no way I can own up to what I did.

Walking over to the other side of the room, Bob seems to be full of the kind of pent-up, tightly wound energy of an angry beast. He paces back and forth, clearly finding it hard to stay calm.

"I swear I locked all the doors," Henry says weakly, close to tears.

"Shut up!" Bob screams, marching over to him and leaning into his face. "Shut the fuck up! I don't want excuses! All the excuses in the world won't bring her back, and now she's gone off to tell her friends all about us! Do you realize the level of danger we're in thanks to your incompetence?!"

"I was -" Henry starts to say.

"Shut up!" Bob screams again, before turning and using the butt of his rifle to smash the window of a display cabinet in the corner of the room. Glass drops own to the floor, followed by a brief moment of calm as Bob walks over to the window and looks out at the dark city. "Think about it," he says after a few seconds. "That bitch is out there somewhere, heading back to her comrades. As soon as she tells them about us, about our supplies, they'll come for us. They might be better armed than us, there might be more of them". He turns to us. "Your incompetence and stupidity might have doomed us all, boy. How does that feel? The blood of your own sister on your hands".

"I'm not dead," I say, starting to get worried about how far Bob's anger might drive him.

"Not yet," Bob says, walking back over to us. "But the risk level has increased dramatically". He pauses for a moment, staring at Henry. "It's my fault," he says eventually. "I'm sorry. I shouldn't have got so angry. It was unprofessional of me. This is my fault as much as anyone's. I never should have given you so much responsibility, Henry. I assumed I could trust you to do the job properly, but clearly that was an error of judgment. It's my fault that you were given a job you couldn't complete".

"I checked the doors," Henry says, with tears streaming down his face. "I checked every door and every window, I swear. They were locked".

"Clearly they weren't," Bob replies, "and the fact that you still won't acknowledge your mistake is another sign that you're too immature to be trusted".

"They -" Henry starts to say.

"Then where is she?" Bob shouts. "Go down there, and show me where that bitch has got to, because she's most certainly not anywhere in this building. What are you suggesting? Did she gnaw through her ropes and then climb out through the mailbox? Did she escape into the air ducts? She's vanished into thin air, and the only possible explanation is that I trusted a foolish little child to secure the building and he let me down!" He states at Henry for a moment, and I can't shake the fear that he might hit him. "Get out of my sight," he sneers eventually. "I can't even stand to look at you. As far as I'm concerned, you're just a waste of space, so get out of here". With that, he turns and walks over to the broken window.

"Henry -" I start to say.

"Fuck off," Henry replies, turning and hurrying back to his room.

Once Henry's gone, I stare at Bob and try to work out what I should say. I know I can't tell him that I'm the one who helped Mallory to get away, but at the same time I feel as if I need to deflect some of his anger away from my brother. Walking slowly across the room, I try to desperately to think of some way that I might be able to calm him down, but ultimately I come up with nothing.

"I'm sorry," Bob says after a moment. "I shouldn't have reacted like that. Your brother's a good kid". He turns to me. "But that's all he is. A kid. He's nothing more than a child, and it was wrong of me to give him so much responsibility. I suppose I just wanted to believe that I could trust him". He sighs. "I'm gonna need your help, Elizabeth. I can't deal with this whole situation alone. Now that the girl is gone, it's more important than ever that we get our act together and work out what we're gonna do. I can't hold everything up together, so I need to know I can count on you".

"I just want to do what's right," I reply.

"As do we all," he says firmly. "As do we

all. That's why I'm going to propose that we discuss the possibility of being more proactive. We need to secure the entire street, at least for now. We need to have some kind of early-warning system in place. I'm not sure what that should be right now, but we have to assess the situation and come up with some kind of plan". He pauses for a moment. "I know you might not necessarily agree with this, but I think it's worth considering the possibility that we should move to a more secure location. Within the city, ideally, but possibly further afield".

"We can't leave New York," I say.

"Because of your parents?"

"Because we're safe here," I tell him.

"We'll talk about this later," he replies, "but Mallory's escape raises the stakes dramatically, and we need to do more than just sit around and wait to be attacked. We need to accept the current reality and work out how best to face the threats that emerge. Otherwise, we risk sleep-walking straight into a lethal situation. There are people out there who'd kill us for our supplies. You understand that, right? They'd walk in here and cut out throats without any hesitation. That's what people get like when they're desperate, when they need food to feed their families. They group together so they can work better, and suddenly the mob mentality takes over and..." His voice trails off for a moment, as if he's lost in thought. "There are only three of us," he continues eventually, "and don't take this the wrong way, but two of you are children. Unless you can both grow up real fast, we have a serious problem".

"But you don't *know* that Mallory is dangerous," I point out. "You don't *know* that she was here to get information about us. She might just be on her own. She might actually have been someone who could have helped us". "I highly doubt that," he replies, heading to the door. "Get some sleep. In the morning, we'll all talk about this, and we'll work out what to do next". With that, he heads out into the corridor, leaving me standing alone in the hallway, trying not to panic. The thought of leaving the building and finding somewhere else to live is terrifying, but the thought of staying with Bob might actually be worse.

THOMAS

Oklahoma

SITTING BY THE SIDE of the road, watching as the sun slowly starts to light the morning sky behind a distant row of trees, I realize I can hear movement in the truck behind me. I guess my brother Joe is waking up from his long, hungover sleep. We've driven all night along the lonely roads that lead to Scottsville, and Joe slept the whole way. I was kinda hoping he wouldn't wake up for a few more hours, but I can hear the door of the truck opening, and now there are footsteps heading slowly toward me over the damp grass.

"What are we doing here?" he asks, sounding groggy.

"Just taking a break," I say.

"Why?"

"Because I've been driving almost twelve hours without stopping".

"Yeah, well..." He wanders over to a nearby tree and starts taking a leak. "I can take over from here, if you like".

"Are you sober?" I ask.

"Sober as a rock," he replies, zipping up and coming back over to me. "Might as well make use of me while you can". He pauses for a moment, apparently waiting to see if I might laugh. "It's a joke, kid. Come on, lighten up".

Taking a deep breath, I continue to just stare at the horizon. I can't stop thinking about the house we left behind, and whether or not it's still burning. All those familiar rooms, with flames ripping through all our possessions, while our mother's dead body was sitting at the kitchen table. For some reason, I keep fixating on her head, and imagining her hair burning away as the flames consumed her body. There's also the fact that I think I saw someone standing in the flames as we drove away. I want to believe I just imagined the whole thing, but there's a part of me that thinks there's maybe a connection between the figure and the dead cop.

"Seen anyone else on the road?" he asks.

I shake my head.

"Figured. Seen any sign of life at all? Planes,

helicopters?"

Again, I shake my head.

"Fuck," he mutters. "They're really leaving us alone to get on with things, aren't they?"

"It doesn't look good," I reply. There's an awkward pause. "Mom said -"

"Let's not talk about Mom," Joe replies, with a firmness in his voice that makes me realize he's determined to block out all mention of what happened yesterday. "We got enough gas?"

"Yes," I say through gritted teeth. "I took care of that. I also made sure we have enough food and water to last a week. We're pretty well stocked up".

He nods. "Good job, boy. I guess I can rely on you after all".

"It's not as if I could leave it to you," I point out.

"So how much longer do you think it's gonna be before we get to Scottsville?" he asks. Typical Joe, always evading the difficult part of the conversation.

"You think we can just get up and get on with things?" I ask, finding it hard to believe how easily he's able to act like nothing's wrong.

"You know," he continues, "there's a good chance we're gonna find help when we get to Scottsville. There's gonna be people there. Scottsville's not big, but it's bigger than our farm, so there's probably some kind of rescue operation going on and there'll be people there. Like, from the government. There'll be information. This isn't the end of the world".

"You don't know that for sure," I say.

"Then there's only one way to find out," he replies, getting to his feet. "Seriously, I can drive for a bit. You need to get some rest". He pats my shoulder. I guess this is his way of being nice.

ELIZABETH

Manhattan

"IT WAS YOU," Henry says, standing in the doorway.

Rolling over in bed, I see that he's staring at me with a dark, pained expression. The first rays of sunlight are starting to come through the window, and a constant breeze is blowing through the apartment thanks to the broken window in the front room.

"What was me?" I ask, my heart racing. I know exactly what he's talking about, but I have to maintain a facade of innocence.

"I know I locked the doors," he continues, "and I know I locked the windows. I know for a fact that I didn't fuck up, so there's only one way they could have been opened. Someone did it on purpose. Someone helped her. Someone betrayed the rest of us. You must have got the key somehow and helped the girl to escape".

I stare at him. I want to tell him the truth, to tell him that we need to stick together and avoid the excesses of Bob's paranoia, but there's something about Henry that worries me. Over the past few days, he's been drawn closer and closer to Bob, and now he seems to be increasingly unstable. It's a hard thing to admit to myself, but I really don't trust my brother anymore.

"Don't even bother to lie," he says. "I've spent the whole night trying to work it out, and there's no other explanation that comes close to making as much sense. I know what you're like, Elizabeth. You care about people. You don't understand the hard choices that have to be made, and you've got this bleeding heart desire to help everyone". He stares at me, with a look on his face that makes it clear that he finds me to be pitiful. "You probably saw her and felt sorry for her. You probably untied the ropes and helped her out the back door. You probably even gave her some of *our* food, and some of *our* water".

"No," I say, even though he's pretty much spot-on. That's exactly what I did.

"So if I go down to our supplies and check," he continues, "I won't find anything missing?"

I pause, trying to work out what to say next. I can't admit the truth to him; he'd go to Bob.

"Or are we supposed to believe that she found the supplies herself?" he asks. "Is that what you thought at the time? You thought you could string together a bunch of unlikely events, and somehow Bob and I would believe them? I guess you must think we're pretty dumb".

"I didn't do anything like that," I say. I feel bad for lying, but I have no choice.

"Whatever".

"It's true!" I insist.

"Liar".

Taking a deep breath, I clear a space on the end of the bed for him. "Come and sit down," I say, figuring it's time I laid my cards on the table for him. There's been so much happening, it's difficult to know who I can trust. At the same time, I figure maybe I should go out on a limb and offer Henry a chance to make the right decision.

"I'm okay over here," he says firmly.

"Do you remember what it was like before all of this happened?" I ask, trying to appeal to the old, pre-Bob version of Henry. "One week ago. Do you remember how things were? You were probably sitting around playing video games -"

"Bullshit," he replies. "I didn't just sit around playing video games. I did so much more other stuff, but you didn't notice. I'm not saying it's your fault, but don't stereotype me as some kind of video game junkie, okay?"

"Okay," I say, taken aback by the level of resentment in his voice. "But life was different back then, wasn't it? We didn't worry about things like our food supply or the danger from people attacking our buildings. We didn't argue about girls tied up in the basement. We didn't have to think about people we found in abandoned cars, and you definitely didn't have to use a rifle to kill them". I pause for a moment. "Are you okay about that, Henry? I mean, you shot that guy -"

"He wasn't a guy," he snaps back at me. "He was a monster".

"He was still a guy," I reply, "and -"

"No!" Henry says firmly, almost shouting. "He *wasn't* a guy! Not in any way! He was a *thing*, just like a fucking animal or something!" He takes a deep breath. "What I shot wasn't a guy, so stop saying that".

"Okay," I reply, realizing that this is a difficult subject for him. "But the point is, Henry, everything has changed in such a short period of time. You've gone from not knowing Bob to being his best friend in, what, four days? Do you really think he's the best person for us to be with right now? There's something about him that makes me worry, Henry. It's as if he's going deeper and deeper into insanity, and he's gonna drag us there with him. We need to break away from all of this, maybe find some other way to get through things. It's like Bob's going crazier every day".

"He's done a lot for us," Henry replies. "Without Bob, we might not even be here right now. He made us address the seriousness of our situation and take actions to keep our supplies safe".

"That's not entirely true," I point out. "It's not like he's saved our lives". "Without Bob, we'd just be sitting targets," he insists. "We'd be sitting here defenseless and helpless, just waiting for someone to come along and take all our food. Without Bob, would we have gone out there and taken supplies from local shops, or would we be sitting on a little pile of stuff that's getting smaller and smaller?"

"But it's changing us," I reply.

"That's a good thing," he says. "Bob's making us grow up. He gave us guns, so we can defend ourselves, and he made it so we can recognize the dangers around us. He changed everything, and we have to stick with him. I know he can be kind of tough at times, but that's what the world's like right now. Bob organizes things and he makes sure we don't just become a pair of kids sitting around in an empty building. We might be dead by now without Bob. You know that, right? He might have saved our lives".

"Do you really believe that?" I ask.

"Yes," he says firmly, "and there's something else I believe. I believe you untied that girl and helped her get out of here. I believe you decided you know better than Bob, and you thought he was being too harsh with her".

"He was torturing her!" I reply, exasperated by the way Henry seems determined to defend Bob at every opportunity.

"He was questioning her," he says, "and he was getting somewhere. He had a plan, but you went and decided you knew better. So now she's out there, and now Bob doesn't trust us, and now you have to accept that if something bad happens, Elizabeth, it's your fault. You don't know that the girl isn't off telling her friends about us right now, and then they'll get all their weapons together and they'll come down here, and they'll kill us, and then they'll take all our stuff and that'll be the end of everything".

"You're paranoid," I say.

"No, you're naive!"

"The world isn't like that -" I start to say.

"It is now!" he shouts. "It's exactly like that, and the only person who knows how to deal with it is..." He pauses. "I get that you have your own ideas," he continues eventually, "but you can't go around interfering with things other people are doing. You can't go around undoing Bob's work. If you'd captured that girl, then maybe you could have been the one to decide what to do with her, but Bob captured her, so it was his choice. You basically stole her from him -"

"You can't steal a person," I reply, although I immediately realize that Bob seems to have 'stolen' Henry from me. I feel as if I can't win this argument without admitting that I helped Mallory to get away, but at the same time I don't feel as if I trust Henry enough to let him know the truth. Given that he probably feels the need to prove himself to his master right now, he'd probably go straight to Bob and tell him what happened. I hate the feeling of not being able to trust my own brother, especially now that he might be the only family I've got left.

"You still won't admit it, will you?" he continues. "You helped that girl to get away from us, but you won't admit it because you know, deep down, that you made a mistake. You know that you let your sympathy for her take over and force you to make a bad choice".

I shake my head.

"Face it," he says, turning to go back through to the rest of the apartment, "you couldn't leave Bob to make the decision. You had to jump in and assume you knew best. I just hope you know that if this all goes wrong... if it turns out that the girl comes back with some other people and we end up losing our supplies, I'm gonna blame you. I'm gonna blame you for everything. You're arrogant. You're self-absorbed. You'd make a really fucking bad solider, Elizabeth".

I sit on the bed and listen to him walking away. Did he really just tell me I'm a bad soldier? Did he just call me arrogant? Bob has clearly got right inside his head, filling him with ideas that make little sense. It's as if he's bought completely into Bob's view of the situation as being some kind of military operation. Taking a deep breath, I realize that I'm totally alone now, with no-one to talk to and no-one who can listen to what I have to say. Even worse, I think I've finally started to give up hope that my parents are ever coming back. For the past few days, I've had this constant belief that eventually they're going to walk back through the door, having made their way here from the airport. But now that belief is gone, and I realize it's just me and Henry. And Bob.

And Mallory. I need to go and talk to Mallory.

THOMAS

Oklahoma

WHEN I WAKE UP, I realize the truck has stopped moving. Looking over at the driver's side, I see an empty seat, and I spot a familiar sight outside. I sit up and realize that we're back at the gas station where we first picked up Lydia a few days ago. For a moment, I wonder whether I'm dreaming, but then I remember that it's perfectly natural for us to come this route on our way into town. I guess I just don't like being reminded of what happened after we were here before.

"Joe!" I shout as I climb out of the truck. Walking over to Lydia's car, I see that it's exactly how she left it. There's even a small suitcase in the back seat. When we left the other day, the plan was for her to come back and get her stuff the next day, but she never made it. Within twenty-four hours, she was sick; within forty-eight hours, she was dead.

"In here!" Joe calls back from inside the building.

Taking a deep breath, I turn and look out across the valley. The whole world seems so still right now, as if a million distant noises have stopped. It's the kind of thing you don't normally notice; it's the background hum of the world, but suddenly it's gone and I'm left with this feeling of being completely alone. What if this is it? What if everyone else is dead, and all that's left is Joe and me?

"What are you doing?" I ask as I walk through the door of the gas station. The place is exactly how it was when we were here the other day, as if no-one's been here since. With no lights, it's gloomy and kind of creepy, and there's a pretty nasty smell coming from some of the rotting food that was left in various cabinets.

"There's still no gas," Joe says, as he wanders the aisles and drops various items into a shopping basket. "I just figured we should stock up. You never know what we'll be able to get in town".

"We've got food," I say. "What we need to do is get to Scottsville".

"I'll only be a couple of minutes," he replies,

grabbing some chocolate bars. "Before you get all preachy on me again, the fresh food is off. Go take a look for yourself. All the sandwiches are covered in fucking mold, so I figure chocolate's better than nothing, right?" He grabs some more bars. "Mom would've fucking freaked out if she could see this, right?"

Heading over to the drinks cabinet, I grab a bottle of water and take a drink. It's kind of warm, since there's no power to the cabinet, but at least it's something. When we left the farm, water was my biggest worry.

Sighing, I grab a basket and fill it with as many bottles of water as possible, and then I follow Joe back out to the truck. From here, it should only take us a few more hours to reach Scottsville, and I can't shake this dark feeling in my gut that maybe we won't like what we find. Lydia said that the place was deserted, but whatever's going on there, it seems to have already swallowed up my father. Climbing into the truck, I realize that Joe has fallen uncharacteristically silent in the past few minutes. I guess he's thinking the same kind of things that I'm thinking, and while we both know that we have to keep going, we're both scared about what we might find when we reach our destination.

ELIZABETH

Manhattan

MAKING MY WAY QUIETLY across the delivery yard, I glance over my shoulder to make absolutely certain that no-one's following me, and then I slip into the maintenance shed at the rear of the adjacent building. It's completely quiet down here, with not even the sound of air-conditioning units to disturb the air; all I can hear are my own footsteps as I carry a small bag of food along a deserted corridor, eventually arriving in what used to be the kitchen for a hotel restaurant. All around me, there are bare silver work-spaces, waiting for cooks and chefs who are never going to come back to work.

The place looks completely empty and abandoned.

"Mallory," I hiss. To be honest, there's a part of me that thinks she won't be here. After all, although she accepted my offer of help when I untied her during the night, I wouldn't blame her if she bolted as soon as I left her alone. Her experience with Bob must have made her extremely wary of strangers, and I'm certain that I'd have run if I was in her position. Still, I've got this lingering fear that if she *has* run, it might mean that Henry and Bob were right; perhaps she's gone to tell someone about us, and perhaps they'll be coming for our supplies.

Just as I'm about to call her name out again, I hear a noise nearby. Turning, I see Mallory emerging from being a doorway. She hurries over to the end of the corridor, as if she's checking that I've come alone.

"I brought you some food," I tell her. "Just like I promised. I'm sorry it took a while, but I had to make sure no-one followed me. It's all a big tense in there right now, but I think it's gonna be okay".

She stares at me, clearly not convinced that she can trust me. She looks to be about my age, although her white-blonde hair makes her seem a little older. There are still some cuts and bruises on her face, which I assume are left over from her encounters with Bob.

"I'll just put this here," I say, placing the bag on the counter. "How are you feeling?"

"Sore," she says, hurrying over and opening the bag. Without saying anything else, she eats the two sandwiches I brought, before washing them down with a small bottle of orange juice. It's like seeing a starved animal devouring its first meal for days, but then I guess Mallory probably didn't get much, if anything, from Bob.

"We don't really have much food," I say. "I don't even know if they'll notice that this stuff's gone, but it should be okay".

Once she's finished eating, Mallory wipes her mouth and takes a few steps back.

"I'm not gonna hurt you," I say. "I just brought you some food 'cause you seemed so hungry. I don't even think I can bring you much more, maybe not until tomorrow. They've noticed you're missing, so you can't come anywhere near the building. They think you're gonna run off and tell some gang all about us. Bob's convinced you're part of some heavily-armed group that wants to come storming into the building and take all our stuff". I pause for a moment. "You're not, are you?"

"That guy's insane," she replies, staring at me wildly.

"I know," I say. "He's got some serious issues. Whatever he did to you -"

"He hasn't got 'serious issues'. He's a fucking psychopath. He's completely off the deep end. You know that, right?"

I nod. "He thinks he's a -"

"Look at my hands," she continues, showing me the crusty, bloodied ends of her fingers. "He told me he'd rip off my fucking fingernails if I didn't tell him about my friends. He kept saying I must have friends; he kept going on and on about it, like he thought the three of you living in that building are the most important people in the whole fucking city. He wanted to know where they were hiding, and how many there were". She pauses for a moment. "At first, he said he wanted to offer them help, but later he said he was going to kill them and take their food. He said that's the kind of world we live in now. He kept telling me over and over again that life isn't fair and that I shouldn't expect it to be. One time, he even tried to come onto me, telling me I should give him things if I wanted him to let me go. I swear to God, if I had the spare energy right now, I'd go right back in there and stick a knife in his gut".

"He's dangerous," I tell her, "but I'm *not*".

"Yeah, well..." Her voice trails off for a moment. "Forgive me for being suspicious, but someone who hangs out with a psychopath clearly has some problems of her own".

"It's not like that," I reply. "We were kind of thrown together. This is just how things are right now".

"And that little helper of his," she says.

"He's just as bad. Beady-eyed little shit".

"Helper?" I pause, realizing she must mean Henry. "That's my brother".

"Well, he's evil," she continues. "He just stood there, watching what the bigger guy was doing to me".

"But he didn't join in, did he?" I ask. "Please. Tell me he didn't join in".

"He helped," she says. "The big guy asked him to fetch stuff, like pliers and things, and the kid went and got them like an obedient little fucker. The big guy took my fingernails off, one by one, and dropped them into this little cup that the kid was holding. I was fucking trying to scream, but I had this gag over my mouth. I kept hoping the kid might come and help me, but he didn't. He just watched and followed orders. So, no, the kid didn't actually do anything, he didn't *actually* touch me, but he sure fucking helped".

"He's not like that," I reply. "He's a good person, he just -"

"You're his sister," she says, interrupting me. "You don't see it, but he's bad". She pauses. "Thanks for your help," she says after a moment, "but I can't stay around here. I have to go".

"Where to?" I ask.

"None of your business".

"Are there other people?"

"That depends on your definition of people,"

she replies. "There's a few people on the other side of town. They're working together. They're gonna head out of the city soon, find somewhere safer. I'm gonna go with them, if it's not too late. I can't stay here. I'll die".

"Where are they gonna go?" I ask.

"They're gonna head west," she says. "That's all they've decided so far. They figure going west is their best chance of finding decent land. I guess the plan is to try growing food, that kind of thing. There's only five or six of us, but we've seen enough of this place to know we can't stay. Not with those things around all the time".

"What things?"

"The things. You must have seen them. Dead people, but they're not quite dead. There's this guy named Kendricks, he's got all kinds of theories. At first, people were saying there were zombies, but Kendricks thinks it's more to do with a virus. I don't really know, but he sounds like he knows what he's talking about. He's the one who thinks we should abandon the city and head out west". She pauses for a moment. "You know, you might be able to come with us, if you want. Kendricks says that anyone who's fit and healthy can be useful".

"I can't leave my brother," I tell her. "And I can't leave New York, not while there's a chance that my parents might show up".

"You're making a mistake," she says. "No-one's coming back. There's not gonna be this big 'on' switch that magically makes everything okay again. That's what I thought for the first couple of days, but eventually I realized there's no chance. The best thing to do is to get into a group and then come up with a plan. Staying in this place is definitely *not* a plan. It's suicide".

"What about your parents?" I ask. "Don't you have family here?"

"They're dead," she replies.

"What happened to them?"

"They got sick, like everyone else got sick. Probably, anyway. I never really..." She pauses. "There's something wrong with this place. We all need to get out".

"I haven't got a choice," I point out.

"You've always got a choice". She sighs. "I have to get going, but thanks for helping me get away. That guy was insane. I'm pretty sure he was gonna kill me". She turns and heads toward the door, before looking back at me. "Do you know the bridge on the north side of Central Park?" she asks suddenly. "The little white one with the old-fashioned lights at each side?"

"Yeah," I say.

"If you change your mind about staying here," she continues, "that's where I'm probably gonna be for a couple more nights, while we get ready to move on".

"I won't change my mind," I tell her.

"I know, but *if* you do, that's where we'll be. Like I said, the original plan was to move out of the city in a couple of days. Until then, we're gonna be gathering stuff together, ready for the journey. It's not much, but it's a start. Just..." She pauses, as if she's not sure whether she can say the next thing. "Just don't bring your brother," she adds finally. "After the stuff that happened here, I don't ever wanna see him again. If you come to the park and you bring him, I won't let him join our group. You understand that, right?"

I nod.

"Seeya around, then," she says. "Or not, most likely". Turning, she heads out the door and I'm left standing alone in the kitchen, listening to the sound of her footsteps as she walks away.

Once she's gone, I turn and look across the kitchen. While I'm here, I figure I might as well check that there's nothing that might be useful. I spend a few minutes going through various cupboards, but the only thing I find is a bunch of cooking pots and some utensils. Eventually, just as I'm about to give up, I spot a door over in the corner, and I find a small pantry. There's not much left in here, but there are a few sachets of powdered soup and some blocks of noodles. I figure I can take this stuff back with me, and at least I'll be able to make Henry and Bob think that I came out scavenging today. Henry, at least, is probably already suspicious of my actions, and I need to make sure I don't do anything to heighten those suspicions. By bringing food to Mallory, I've already taken a huge risk. Now I just need to find a way to make Henry realize that Bob's a bad influence, and then I need to work out what the hell we're going to do next.

THOMAS

Oklahoma

"I DON'T SEE ANYTHING," Joe says, staring out the windshield of the parked truck. "Do you?"

"Looks dead to me," I reply.

We sit in silence for a moment. Ahead of us, the first few buildings of Scottsville sit in ominous silence. There's no sign of life, no sign of movement. There's nothing. It's like the whole place is abandoned, although we haven't actually dared to make our way into the center of town. Scottsville's a small place with just a couple of hundred residents, so it's not like it should be a hive of activity. Still, there's something about the place, even when viewed from outside, that seems strangely subdued.

"I don't hear anything, either," I say, rolling

down my squeaky window. "Listen. There's no sound of anything".

"What do you think?" Joe asks. "Do we carry on, or do we go around?"

I take a deep breath, trying to work out what we should do next. For the past few days, the answer has always been easy: go to Scottsville. Although I could tell that something serious had happened, I was always able to fool myself into believing that going to Scottsville would somehow make things okay. I lied to myself and imagined there being people here; people who'd know what had happened, people who could explain everything, people who could tell us what to do next. If I'm honest, I guess I was relying on there being someone in Scottsville who could wave a magic wand and make it seem like everything would be okay again.

I was wrong.

"I mean, we can just carry on," Joe says after a moment. "We can head on to Dudley. How far's that? Another fifty, sixty miles? It's not so much more. Maybe there are people in Dudley who -"

"Why would there be people in Dudley when there's no-one in Scottsville?" I ask. "Scottsville's bigger than Dudley".

"Okay, so we carry on until we hit Oklahoma City if we have to. Tulsa, maybe".

"And what if there's no-one there, either?"

He sighs. "If there's no-one in Oklahoma City? Then we're fucking screwed. I mean, people don't just vanish. They have to physically be somewhere. There's no magic trick in the world that can take all the people out of Oklahoma City and just make them all disappear".

I stare at the buildings up ahead. After all this planning, we can't just drive around the place and not stop to see what's been happening. "We need to go through the main street," I say, turning to Joe. "Let's just drive through slowly. We can always speed up and get out of there if there's any kind of problem, but we need to see what's happening. Lydia said it was empty. Let's go through the middle and take a look".

"Okay," he says, "but at the first sign of trouble, I'm flooring the pedal. You got me? I'm not wasting a fucking second". Without another word, he starts the engine, and we drive slowly past the first houses. "You see anything?"

I shake my head. The truth is, Scottsville looks deader than dead. I can't put my finger on it, but something about the place just seems totally still and undisturbed, as if no-one's been here for days. It's almost as if a faint layer of dust has descended on the whole town, and there was no-one around to clean up. As the truck continues to move slowly along the street, it's hard not to think about what might be inside these houses. After all, people don't just disappear, and there could be bodies hidden just out of sight. Eventually, Joe takes a left turn and we reach the main street, which is wider than the others but just as deserted. Where once there would have been a few people wandering from store to store, now there's nothing but a few abandoned cars and a whole lot of dust.

"Lydia wasn't kidding," Joe says as we drive slowly past the convenience store. "Look at this place. Middle of the day, and there's no-one about. Where the hell did everyone go?"

"Maybe they were evacuated," I reply.

"By who?"

"The military. Maybe the army came through and rounded everyone up. I guess they missed us 'cause our farm's so far out".

"We'd have heard," he says. "We'd have seen helicopters or something. Somehow, we'd know what was going on".

"It's the most likely explanation," I say. "What else could have happened? You think everyone just upped and died in their houses?"

"Maybe," he says, suddenly parking up in the middle of the street. "So do you think we should go take a look around? There might be some decent food in the store".

"I thought you didn't want to get out of the truck," I remind him.

"Doesn't look too dangerous," he says with a shrug. "I don't see no rampaging hoards, do you?"

"No," I say, "but I saw the cop back at the -"

"For fuck's sake, will you knock that off?" he says. "I don't know what you saw when you found that cop, but I'm damn sure you're confused about the whole thing. Dead cops don't just crawl around, okay? This isn't a zombie movie, there's no aliens coming down from space. Whatever happened, it was something weird but it wasn't something crazy. Look at this place. It's totally empty".

Staring out at the storefronts, I feel a knot in my stomach as I consider what it might be like in there. I feel like there's a really good chance that we'll find dead bodies, and I'm also worried about that cop from yesterday. If he could keep moving even after he seemed to be dead, there's no reason why others couldn't have done the same. Then again, if the two hundred people of Scottsville were in a similar state, I guess we'd have seen some kind of a sign by now.

"You can wait here if you want," Joe says, getting out of the truck. "I'm gonna go take a look in the store".

"I'll come," I reply quickly, getting out and following him across the dusty street. I keep glancing over my shoulder, expecting to see someone or something.

"So," Joe continues as we reach the store and find that the door is locked, "you got any moral objections if I break this thing down?"

I shake my head.

"Cool," he says, standing back. "If this goes well, I might even try busting down the door of the bank later. I've always wanted to be an old-fashioned highwayman". With that, he runs at the door of the convenience store, which gives way easily. A thin cloud of dust immediately floats out into the afternoon air, along with a foul smell that I can only hope comes from nothing more grizzly than some rotten fruit.

"I don't think there's gonna be anything in there," I say, keen to stay outside.

"We've gotta check," Joe replies, stepping through the door. "I'll just be a couple of minutes".

Part of me wants to go in with him, but I find myself loitering out in the street. It's weird being here when there's no-one else around. I must have been to Scottsville a hundred times, and I always thought it was a dead little place. It never seemed like anything was actually happening here, and I always dreamed of heading off somewhere to experience a real town, or even a city. Suddenly, though, I find myself desperately wanting the old Scottsville back. I just want to see one person come around the corner.

"There's nothing in there," Joe says,

emerging from the store. "All the fresh stuff's rotten, and it's not like we need more chocolate, right?"

"Did you find anyone?" I ask.

He shakes his head.

"Did you look behind the counter?"

"Of course I looked behind the counter. There's no-one in there". He walks across the street, before stopping to look around. "What the fuck happened to this place?" he asks, before cupping his hands around his mouth. "Hello?" he shouts at the top of his voice. "Is there anyone still here?"

"Don't do that!" I say, hurrying over to him.

"Why not?" he asks.

"What if there's people here we don't want to see?"

"Like who?" He pauses for a moment. "Are you still banging on about that cop? Thomas, you're letting your imagination run away with you. Does it really seem like there's gonna be a bunch of fucking zombies sitting around this place? It's dead as all hell. The only chance is that maybe there's some people holed up somewhere and they're asleep. I don't wanna just drive through and maybe miss the chance of making contact".

"A few minutes ago, you didn't want to drive through at all," I point out.

"Let's not do this," he replies, walking over to the other side of the street.

"Do what?" I ask, following him.

"Arguing's a waste of time," he says as we walk along the sidewalk. "It's a waste of fucking energy, too. Let's just get on with doing what we need to do, like -" He stops in front of a bar and grabs the handle; the door swings open, revealing a dark interior. "What do you know?" he says, turning to me. "At least there's one place that's still open".

"You're not serious," I reply. "There's no way you're serious".

"Relax," he says, pulling the door shut. "Even I'm not dumb enough to think we should stop for a drink. But I'll be damned if I'm not curious about what happened here. It's like someone just came along and sucked up all the people. A whole town doesn't just disappear like this". We start walking again, making our way to the end of the street. "There's got to be someone here," he continues. "There's got to be someone, somewhere, who knows what the fuck is going on. I refuse to believe that the whole fucking town of Scottsville has just upped and vanished overnight. There's someone somewhere, I swear to God, and we're gonna find them".

Just as he finishes speaking, there's a noise in the distance. It's not much, and it only lasts a couple of seconds, but it sounded like something hitting a piece of metal. Joe and I exchange a worried glance, and we stand in silence for a moment, waiting for the noise to return.

"It was probably just the wind," Joe says eventually, his voice filled with tension.

"There's no wind," I reply.

"We're going back to the truck," he says, grabbing my arm and starting to pull me back the way we came. We only get a few steps along the street, however, before we both spot the same thing up ahead: a figure, climbing into our truck.

"Oh shit, no," Joe says, fumbling through his pockets, just as we hear the truck's engine start up. "Hey!" he shouts, racing toward the vehicle, but it's too late. With screeching tires, the truck shoots forward and veers straight around Joe before speeding off down the street, leaving us both in the dust.

ELIZABETH

Manhattan

AFTER DOUBLE-CHECKING THAT THERE'S no-one nearby, I pull the key from my pocket and slip it into the lock on the front door of Harrison Blake's apartment.

Or, at least, that's what I *try* to do, because no matter how hard I try to get it to the fit, the key just won't go into the hole. After a couple of seconds, I suddenly realize that the lock has changed. Before, it was a scratched and old silver lock, but now it's shining new and gold. Before I can really react properly, I hear the sound of someone turning the handle from within, and the door opens to reveal Bob's smiling face.

"Good afternoon," he says politely. "Can I

help you?"

"I just..." I look down at the key in my hand, and it's immediately clear that the game is up. "I just came to look for a book," I say, deciding to play it cool. After all, now that Bob seems to have found the books, I guess my best option is to pretend that I thought he knew all along.

"Well," Bob says, with a curious glint in his eyes, "the books aren't up here anymore. Henry and I took them down to the storage rooms. I figured books are a valuable resource right now, so we need to make sure they're safe. After all, it's not as if we can just go online and look for information, is it?"

"No," I stammer, my mind racing as I try to think of a way out of this situation. "Well," I continue after a moment, "I guess I'll just go and look downstairs for a -"

"Not so fast," Bob says. "Where did you get that key?"

"Harrison Blake gave it to me," I reply.

"When?"

"The other day, before he left".

"Why didn't you mention it?"

"I didn't think it was important. You've got a master-key to the whole building anyway, so... I assumed it wasn't an issue".

"You did, did you?" he asks, stepping out of the apartment and pulling the door shut. "So you had this key to Blake's apartment, and you figured there was no need to share the existence of all these books with the rest of us because... you assumed we already knew?"

I nod.

"I see". He stares at me for a moment. "So it's not like you decided to keep the books from your brother and myself for any other reason. It's not like you chose to deceive us, is it?"

I shake my head.

"That's good," he replies, starting to walk along the corridor toward the stairwell. "Nevertheless, it's hard to interpret this little incident as anything other than a slight against both your brother and myself. Elizabeth, will you accompany me down to the lobby, please?"

"I was going to take a nap," I reply.

"You can do that after you've come to the lobby with me," he says, heading through to the stairwell.

Figuring I have no alternative, I traipse after him. It's pretty clear that he's pissed off about the fact that I kept the existence of all those books from him, but I don't see why he's quite *so* mad; after all, he had a key all along, so it's not my fault that he didn't bother to come up and see if Blake left anything useful behind. At the same time, I can understand how, in his paranoid state, Bob might interpret my actions as some kind of threat. Maybe I should have been smarter and just let him know about the books, but I didn't realize that he felt he had to know everything about the entire building. I'm starting to realize more and more that this entire place is being run according to a new set of rules, and these rules are entirely decided by Bob.

Following Bob down the stairwell, I start to consider my options. The gun Bob gave me is up in my parents' apartment, and the only way out of the building is through the main door at the front of the lobby, or one of the doors at the rear. I keep telling myself that I'm over-reacting and that there's no reason to be so scared, but at the same time I feel as if Bob is consistently moving further and further away from sanity. At least Henry has a rifle, though, so I know Bob can't go completely insane.

"Our little group operates on trust," Bob says as we emerge into the lobby, where Henry is sitting by the door with his rifle poised, reading for any intruders. "I have to know I can trust you," Bob continues, turning to me, "just as you have to know you can trust me. When that trust breaks down, we have a problem, and when we have a problem, we have to rectify things". He pauses for a moment, clearly enjoying the sound of his own voice. "Now, ordinarily, I wouldn't view a lie of omission as a particularly serious thing. Sure, Elizabeth, you should have told us about the books in Harrison Blake's apartment, but I can let that slide. There are other things, though, that I can't let slide".

"Like what?" I ask, my chest tightening as I realize Bob might know more than I'd realized.

"I've been thinking about Mallory," he says, "and how she escaped. You were very keen to let me believe that your brother left a door open, weren't you? But what if that's not what happened? What if your lack of loyalty to this building extended to other actions? When I found your little hideout in Harrison Blake's apartment, Elizabeth, I started to wonder what else you might be keeping from us".

"I didn't -" I start to say.

"I started to think about you as a person," he continues, interrupting me. "I started to wonder what kind of person you are. After all, until a few days ago, I'd never even given you a second thought. So I thought about whether I could trust you, and I came to a startling conclusion. I decided that, when it comes to it, I *can't* trust you. Not for a second. And do you want to know why I can't trust you? It's simple. I believe you released Mallory, and I believe you gave her some food from our dwindling stockpile, and I believe you did all of this despite knowing that both your brother and I have been working to neutralize the threat that she posed -"

"You mean by torturing her?" I ask. As soon as the words have left my lips, I realize I should have kept quiet.

"Here's the thing," Bob says. "At first, I thought that perhaps my suspicions regarding your behavior were unfounded, Elizabeth. I berated myself for thinking so little of someone I barely knew. So I turned to the one person who knows you properly. I asked your brother if he believed you might be responsible for Mallory's escape. I expected him to defend you. I expected him to uphold your honor and tell me I was wrong. But that's not what he did. No, he told me he'd been thinking the same thing. Your own brother, and he couldn't defend you. It hurt me, Elizabeth. It really hurt me to see the anguish in this boy's eyes as he admitted, not in words but in more subtle ways, that he knew you'd betrayed us both".

"Henry," I say, stepping past Bob, "we need to get out of here. Let's go and talk, we need to -"

"Fuck off," he says, staring at the window. It's as if he's refusing to even look at me.

"Henry -"

"Fuck off," he says again, his voice sounding calm and dispassionate. "I don't need you to tell me what to do, and I don't need your help. Bob's right. You let me take the blame for something you did. I can't forgive you for that".

"Bob was *torturing* her!" I say. "He was hitting her, and cutting her. He was pulling out her fingernails, Henry. He was -"

"I know," Henry replies firmly.

"And you just stood there and let him?"

"She came to spy on us," Henry replies, still refusing to look at me. "I trusted Bob, just like I trusted you. The difference is, *he* didn't let me down".

"I didn't let you down," I say.

"What about this morning?" he asks. "What about when you let Bob think I was responsible for Mallory getting away?"

Sighing, I realize I made a huge mistake earlier today. I should have told them both what I'd done; instead, I played right into Bob's hands. "I'm sorry," I say after a moment, "but you can't let that one mistake cloud your judgment, Henry. This man is a psychopath. He's insane! He's -"

"Standing right behind you," Bob says suddenly, sounding rather amused by everything I'm saying. "Now, don't get me wrong, Elizabeth, but I'm starting to get a little insulted by some of the things you're saying. I mean, I consider myself to have a fairly thick skin, but you're throwing some rather nasty accusations around. If you don't like my methods, and if you don't like the way things are run around here, maybe you oughta reconsider your options".

"What the fuck does that mean?" I ask.

"It means you're not welcome here," Bob continues. "We've discussed the matter, and we've voted on it, and we've decided that we're going to ask you to leave".

"You're going to *what*?" I ask, staring at him.

"You heard me. When you helped Mallory get away, you chose your side. You made us realize we can't trust you. That's your choice, and you're perfectly entitled to do whatever you want, but we don't have to suffer the presence of a traitor in our midst".

"Do you hear this guy?" I say, turning to Henry. "Listen to him. He's lost his mind. Can't you see? Bob's insane. He thinks we're in some kind of war! He's obviously watched too many movies! He's not like a -"

"You need to leave," Henry says suddenly, still staring at the door.

"What?" I ask, suddenly feeling a cold sweat pass through my body. "Henry -"

"Bob's right," he continues. "You let us down. We can't trust you. How do we know you won't do the same thing again? How do we know you haven't already agreed to help Mallory and the others? You might sneak down during the night and let them in".

"This is bullshit," I say, almost shaking with anger at the way Bob has managed to turn my own brother against me. How the hell did I let this happen?

"Regardless of your thoughts on the matter," Bob says, "I'm going to invite you to leave the building now". He walks over and opens the door. "I don't feel that we owe you any resources from our supplies, but I'm confident you'll be able to find food nearby, and your new friends will undoubtedly give you something".

"This isn't *your* building," I point out. "You're not in charge".

"Am I not?" he asks, smiling.

"You can't throw me out!" I turn to Henry. "Come on, stop messing about. You know this is insane!"

"You know what?" Bob says, walking over to me. "You're right. This isn't my building. I don't have the authority to throw you out. But then... What are you gonna do to stop me?" He grabs my arm. "We can do this the easy way, Elizabeth, or we can do this the unpleasant way. It's entirely up to you".

"Henry -" I start to say.

"We can't trust you," Henry replies.

"You heard your brother," Bob says.

"Get off!" I shout, trying to get free of his grip. Suddenly, Bob reaches around and puts me in a headlock, before dragging me across the lobby. I push against him, trying to get free, but he quickly gets me out onto the sidewalk, where he throws me down onto the street before hurrying back inside and locking the door.

"Henry!" I shout, getting up and finding that

I'm covered in dust and soot from the sidewalk. "Henry, for God's sake, you can't do this!" I walk over to the door and try to push it open, but the lock is in place. "Henry! Let me in!"

"You're not one of us anymore," Henry shouts back at me. "You made the decision to join the others. So go and join them".

"I'm your sister," I point out.

"All the doors are locked," Bob says, before Henry has a chance to answer. "There's no way for you to get inside. If you think you can indoctrinate your little brother and make him feel sorry for you, you're wrong. That's simply not going to happen. I'd suggest you go to your new friends, Elizabeth, because you'll get nothing from us. We don't give second chances to traitors. If you think our resolves will soften, you're mistaken".

"I'm not going anywhere!" I shout at him. "You can't just throw me out like this! This isn't your building, to decide who's allowed inside and who isn't. It's as much mine and Henry's. There's no way I'm going anywhere until you open this door!"

"Then you'll be stuck out there for a long time," Bob replies. "Looks like rain's on the way, too. If I were you, I'd accept the situation and try to find my pals. Then again, maybe they won't be so interested in you anymore, not when they find out that you can't help them get to us. You've burned your bridges here, Elizabeth. There's no amount of shouting and banging you can do to get back in. When trust is lost, it's lost and there's nothing you can do to win it back". He turns to Henry/ "Boy, I reckon it's time to go and make some new plans. There's been a big of a shake-up and we need to make sure we adapt to the new situation. That's one of the key aspects of this new world. We have to adapt and make sure we meet the current threat. This door's secured. Let's get into the office and work out where we're gonna go from here".

Obediently, Henry turns and walks across the lobby, heading for the office at the back of the building.

"Come back!" I shout as Bob goes to join him. "You can't leave me out here! You can't just toss me out like this!"

Ignoring me, they disappear from sight and I'm left standing alone in the empty street.

"Hey!" I yell, banging on the door. "Henry! Let me in!"

THOMAS

Oklahoma

"WHAT THE FUCK?!" I shout as Joe races past me, trying to catch up to the truck. "Joe!"

"Fuck!" Joe shouts as he trips and falls to the ground, bouncing along the dirt until he comes to a halt. By the time I've caught up to him, the truck is long gone, and we can hear it getting further and further away.

"Were the keys in the ignition?" I ask, stunned.

"Of course the fucking keys were in the ignition," Joe says, trying to catch his breath. "How was I supposed to know someone was gonna come along and steal the fucking thing?"

"Did you see who took it?" I ask.

He shakes his head.

Turning, I look along the dusty, empty street. "Now what?" I ask. "What the fuck are we gonna do now?"

"Don't panic," Joe says. "We'll be okay. We'll just have to find another vehicle, and then I can -".

Suddenly he stops as we both hear a distant sound. It's like the motor of a vehicle, in fact it's like the motor of *our* vehicle, except instead of getting further away, it seems to be getting a little closer. We stand and listen as it seems to pass a few streets away.

"Come on!" Joe says, racing off along a short alley that leads away from the main part of town. We spring along a couple of smaller side roads until Joe pulls up short and grabs my arm. "There," he says, pointing down another street to where our truck is sitting outside a small house. "Son of a bitch," he says, starting to march over there, just as a guy runs out of the house and shoves some boxes into the back of the vehicle.

"Joe -" I start to say.

"Hey!" Joe shouts as we reach the truck. "What the fuck do you think you're doing?"

As soon as he sees us, the guy gets back into the truck. Before he can get going again, however, Joe pulls the passenger-side door open and leaps inside, grabbing the guy and dragging him across the seat. They struggle for a moment, before Joe finally hauls the guy out of the truck and dumps him down to the ground.

"You like our truck?" Joe shouts, pressing his foot against the guy's face. "Huh? You like our truck? You *want* our truck, do you?"

"Joe, don't hurt him," I say.

"Don't hurt him?" Joe laughs. "You hear that, pal? My little brother wants me to not hurt you. He wants me to be all nice to you, despite the fact that you tried to steal our vehicle". Turning, Joe walks a couple of paces away, before coming back and kicking the guy hard in the gut; the guy curls up into a ball and tries to toll away. "This is what we do to people like you," Joe continues, kicking the guy hard in the back.

"That's enough!" I say, pushing Joe back.

"You're lucky my brother's here," Joe spits at the guy, "or I swear to God, I'd kick your fucking head off". He climbs back into the truck, switches the engine off, and removes the key from the ignition. "Do you get this guy, Thomas?" he asks, getting out of the truck and walking around to the back of the vehicle. "Thinks he can just come along and take our property. Now let's see what we've got here". He opens the boxes that the guy placed on the truck. "Food. Some water. Not bad. I guess you had it all figured out, huh? Only problem is, you didn't keep going. If you'd just kept your foot down, you'd be long gone and we'd never have seen you again. Unfortunately, that's not what you did". He comes back over to the guy and, before I can stop him, he kicks him in the back of the head.

"Stop it!" I shout, pushing Joe away. "You're gonna kill him!" Turning, I see that the guy is trying to get to his feet, although he seems dizzy. After a moment, he collapses back onto the side of the truck, and he seems to be having trouble getting his bearings.

"What's your name?" I ask.

The guy blinks a couple of times, as if he's a little spaced out.

"You'd better answer my brother," Joe calls over to him, "or he'll stand aside and we'll go back to doing this my way!"

"Clyde!" the guy shouts over at us, sounding as if he's having trouble breathing. "Clyde Langman, okay? My name's Clyde Langman!" He leans over and spits some blood onto the ground. "I think you fucking broke a couple of my ribs!"

"Did I?" Joe asks. "Shit, I was aiming to so much more fucking damage. Maybe I should try again?"

"Why did you try to take our truck?" I ask.

"I'm sorry," Clyde replies, standing up straight. He's a middle-aged guy, slightly overweight and with a receding hairline. "I swear to God, I just panicked. You're the first people I've seen for days. I just really needed to get out of here, and when I saw your truck with the key still in the ignition... I didn't know if I could trust you, so I just decided to take it".

"Why didn't you just come over and talk to us?" I ask.

"I didn't know who you were," he says. "I didn't even know if you were normal or not".

"Why wouldn't we be normal?" I say.

"Where have you been?" he asks. "Seriously, have you been living under a fucking rock? Where'd you come from, anyway?"

"We live out of town," I tell him. "It took us the best part of half a day to get here".

"How are things out there?" Clyde continues. "Is it like it is here?"

"People are dead," I say. "Lots of people. Everyone's dead, apart from us. They got sick. That's why we came here, 'cause we thought maybe we could find out what's been going on".

"I haven't got any answers for you," Clyde says. "It all started almost a week ago. People started getting sick, and then it all happened really, really fast. Like, first a couple of people were ill, and then within an hour it was almost everyone. I swear to God, I've never seen anything like it. I thought I was the only one left".

"And why does that give you the right to take our truck?" Joe asks.

"It doesn't," Clyde says. "I swear, I've never taken anything before in my entire life, but I just wanted to get out of here. And then I thought I should swing around and get some more supplies from my house, but you..." He pauses for a moment. "Well, I guess the game's up. You got me. I'm sorry".

"Where were you gonna go?" I ask.

He shrugs. "I was just gonna keep driving until I found somewhere. I swear, this was all just a sudden rush for freedom that went really, really wrong. I should've spoken to you. I should've just come right out with it all, instead of trying to steal your truck".

"So you're the only one here?" I ask, still suspicious of his motives.

"There were some others," he says. "Not many, but a few. They died. They got sick and they died. I ended up hiding out, hoping someone might show up. I tried hot-wiring some vehicles, but I didn't really know what I was doing. I was starting to think I'd have to try hiking to the next town, and then I heard your truck".

"We can't stay here," Joe says, sounding impatient. "This place is dead. We have to keep going".

"I want to come with you," Clyde says.

"No way," Joe says firmly.

"We can't just leave him here!" I say, turning

to see that my brother is already getting into the truck.

"He's not our problem," Joe replies. "An extra person is an extra mouth that needs extra food and extra water. He's extra weight, too. He'll slow us down".

"I have my own supplies," Clyde says, hurrying around to the boxes he placed on our trucks. "I have enough to share. I mean, it's the least I can do after the mis-understanding earlier". He pauses for a moment. "Listen, guys, I know we got off on the wrong foot, but I hope you can see past my mistakes and accept my apologies for what happened. I really think we can work together. After all, three heads are better than two, right? And if we're all going in the same direction, why not pool our resources"/

"Give us one good reason," Joe says, clearly not buying the idea for a second.

"Well, I can drive," Clyde says, smiling eagerly. "I can share my resources, like I said. And I've got a plan. At least, the beginning of a plan. I can't do it without you, but I don't think you can do it without me, either".

"What's the plan?" I ask.

He opens his mouth to reply, and then he seems to change his mind. "It's not something I can really explain," he says eventually. "It's more something I have to show you. Basically, would you guys be interested if I told you that I know where there's a classified military base less than a hundred miles from here? If we're looking for answers, I'm pretty sure that's where we should be headed".

DAYS 5 TO 8

DAY 7

ELIZABETH

Manhattan

WALKING ALONG FIFTH AVENUE at 5am, the only sound I hear is my footsteps on the empty sidewalk.

The sound of the city at night used to be: sirens blaring; traffic roaring; horns honking; people talking and laughing and arguing; phones ringing; adverts screaming for attention; the distant boom of airliners; hundreds of other little noises that you never even noticed and that you couldn't have explained anyway.

Tonight, the sound of the city is this: nothing. Just my footsteps, and occasionally the fluttering of a gentle breeze.

An empty city is a terrifying thing. It immediately says: something's wrong. Something's happened. I keep looking up at the dark buildings and wondering where everyone went. Are their bodies inside, rotting in office that used to be air-conditioned? Or did most of them run away in some kind of overnight evacuation that a few of us missed? It's hard to believe that the citizens of New York would have tidied themselves neatly into their office and homes to die, but I guess it's not impossible. Either way, I feel like I'm the only person in the entire city right now.

I'm not, though.

I'm not alone.

As I reach the edge of Central Park, I immediately spot a light in the distance. Flickering behind some trees, it's the light of a small campfire, and right now it's the greatest thing I've ever seen. I glance over my shoulder, somehow unable to shake the feeling that perhaps Henry will have changed his mind and come after me. After all, he's my brother and he has to realize eventually that he's made the wrong choice. But there's no sign of him. The empty street yawns out of the darkness, and I feel a cold shiver pass through my body.

The white bridge. That's where Mallory said she'd be. I make my way into the park and start walking to where I *think* she meant. After a couple of minutes, I realize that I'm obediently sticking to the paths rather than cutting across the grass; even though I know there's no-one around to yell at me for doing the wrong thing, I decide to remain on the path even if it takes me longer. Somehow, it just feels right to do things like this. Besides, I'm worried about getting lost in the dark; with only the moonlight to guide me, I could easily end up wandering around for hours, especially now that it's clear the small fire is just a burning bin sitting out alone in the open.

Eventually, however, I spot another light up ahead, and I see the small white bridge illuminated by a welcoming orange glow from the other side. Picking up the pace slightly, I hurry along the path, ignoring the constant clicks and purrs that I imagine in the darkness. When I get to the bridge, I realize I can hear voices, and soon I see them: a dozen or so people, huddled around a burning oil drum, locked in what seems to be a pretty animated group discussion. As I get closer, I spot Mallory, sitting slightly back from the others and looking as if she doesn't quite belong. I stop and stare at her, and I can't help but wonder whether it was a mistake to come here.

"Elizabeth!" she calls out, suddenly looking over at me. Running down the side of the bridge, she throws her arms around me, acting as if she's pleased to see me. I can barely see her in the darkness, and frankly I'm a little taken aback by her enthusiasm. "I didn't think you'd come," she says, letting go and stepping back. "Are you okay?"

I nod.

"You don't look okay".

I take a deep breath. "Is anyone *okay* right now?"

She smiles and grabs my hand, leading me over to the others. "You can tell me later," she whispers, with a knowing look in her eyes. "Hey, guys! This is Elizabeth! Remember I told you about her? She's the one who helped me get away from the guy who tied me to a fucking chair. I told you she might come and say hi, and now here she is!"

"Is that right?" says a man nearby, as he stands up and walks toward me. "We've heard a lot about you over the past day, Elizabeth. Mallory says you saved her life".

"Oh," I reply, a little taken aback. "I don't know if that's quite what happened".

"I'm pretty sure it is," Mallory says.

"Not many people can say they saved another person's life," the guy continues, reaching out and shaking my hand. "My name's Jonathan Kendricks".

"He's our leader," Mallory says.

"I'm not sure that's quite accurate," Kendricks says with a smile. "We don't have a leader here".

"He's being modest," Mallory adds. "This is

the guy who helped up come up with a plan. Without him, we wouldn't all be working together like this".

"There's strength in numbers," Kendricks continues. "Everyone has a strength. They just have to find it and acknowledge it, and then bring it to the fore". He steps aside and indicates the group of people gathered around the fire. "Won't you join us, Elizabeth? It's not much, but we're more than happy to share".

Smiling awkwardly, I hurry closer to the fire. There's a part of me that hates the idea of coming here and immediately letting these people help me; at the same time, the walk to Central Park was so cold, I feel like I'm on the verge of hypothermia. As I warm myself, I look over at the other people gathered nearby and I realize they're all staring at me with different expressions; there's an older man who looks shocked by my appearance, and a younger guy who looks as if he's a little suspicious, and a middle-aged woman who looks too tired to really give a damn. I can't help wondering if some of them are a little resentful of the way I've just shown up and started warming myself by their fire.

"Ask her," says one of the others suddenly.

"She's not," Mallory says.

"Ask her!" says another person gathered around the fire.

"She's not!" Mallory says again, raising her voice.

"It's okay," Kendricks says, stepping closer to me. "I'll do it". He smiles. "Elizabeth, there's something I need to ask you. As you might be aware, there's a kind of virus going around. We're not absolutely certain about how it works or even what it does, and so far it seems as if it's not easily transmissible to a certain group of people, but we still need to be sure, so..." He pauses for a moment. "Are you sick, Elizabeth?"

"No," I say.

"Are you sure? Do you have any symptoms of anything at all? Coughing? Fatigue? Any kind of rash?"

I shake my head.

"We should check her," says one of the others.

"It's okay," Kendricks says, "I can deal with it. Elizabeth, Mallory says you've been in close contact with some other people. Your brother and another man, is that right?"

I nod.

"Did either of *them* show any sign of sickness?"

"No".

"Nothing at all?"

"Nothing".

"And you're sure you don't feel sick?"

"I'm sure".

He narrows his eyes as he stares silently at me for a moment. "Then that's good enough for me," he says eventually.

"What if she's a carrier?" one of the other voices asks.

"If the virus was passed on so easily, we'd all be dead by now," Kendricks replies. "Do you really have to have this same discussion every time someone new arrives? We talked about all of this two days ago when Susan joined us". He turns to Mallory. "Give her some food. She looks like she's about to faint".

"I'm not tired," I reply. Frankly, I feel so strung out and wired, I don't know if I'll ever be able to sleep again.

"But you're hungry, right?" he continues.

I nod.

"Mallory, take her over to the stash and give her something to eat before she collapses".

"Wait," says another man. "She's our visitor now? Since when did we start giving away food?"

"It's just one sandwich," Kendricks replies.

"She wants to eat, she can find her own food," says one of the women. "What if a hundred people show up? Are we gonna feed them too?"

"We'll take a vote on it," says the other guy. "If you're in favor of giving this girl one of our sandwiches, raise your hand". No hands are raised.

"If you're not in favor," he continues, "raise your hand". Half a dozen hands are raised. "Sorry, girl," the guy says, turning to me. "We're not giving you any of our food".

"Then she can have one of mine," Kendricks says. "Mallory, get a sandwich for Elizabeth and mark it off from my rations".

"Come on," Mallory says, grabbing my hand and leading me away from the group. "Ignore them," she says quietly. "Some of them are fucked in the head, and Kendricks is getting high on his own sense of importance".

"It's fine," I say. "I get it. Food's scarce. You can't just go handing out what you've got to everyone who wanders along".

"That's why we're getting out of here," she replies with a smile. "And you're coming with us".

THOMAS

Oklahoma

"WHAT DO YOU MEAN?" I ask, using my arm to shield my eyes from the sun as I look over at Joe.

"I *mean* it won't start," he replies, leaning under the hood of the truck. "Just give me a minute..."

It's just after sunrise and we were supposed to be heading out of Scottsville, but now it seems that the truck - which was working perfectly well last night - has suddenly developed a fault. To say that this is suspicious timing would be an understatement; to be honest, it's stretching credulity to believe that this particular, hitherto totally reliable truck would go wrong just when we need it the most.

"Is the battery dead?" I ask.

"It's not the battery," he says, sounding annoyed.

"Is it the clutch?"

"No".

"Is it the alternator?"

"No!"

"Is it the -"

"Do you know how to fix stuff like this?" he asks, interrupting me.

"No," I say.

"So you're just randomly asking if it's things you've heard of?"

I pause for a moment. "I was just trying to help".

"Then leave it to someone who *does*. Make yourself useful. Go fetch me something to eat".

Sighing, I turn and walk around to the back of the truck, where our food is stashed in bags, covered by a tarpaulin. Something about this whole situation feels really wrong, and I can't stop wondering whether Clyde Langman has something to do with the problem that's hit the truck. After all, it was Clyde who persuaded Joe and me to stay for the night, and it was Clyde who made a half-hearted attempt to steal the truck yesterday. There's something about that guy that I don't trust, and I can tell Joe's skeptical as well.

"How can it just stop working?" I call back

to Joe.

"I don't fucking know," he replies. "If I knew, I could fix it, couldn't I?"

"You guys got a problem?" Clyde asks, as he steps out of his front door. "I found an old ether cylinder you might be able to use".

"Truck won't start," I say, as I carry a piece of bread over to Joe.

"Won't start?" Clyde hurries over to join us. "What do you mean, it won't start? It was working perfectly fine yesterday!"

"We know," Joe mutters darkly.

"Maybe it's the fuel pick-up," Clyde suggests.

"Great," Joe mutters, "now there's two of 'em".

"Joe's good with vehicles," I tell Clyde. "It's what he's best at".

"Shut up," Joe replies. He pauses for a moment. "Part of being good with stuff is knowing when to try a different approach. I keep thinking that maybe we should just abandon the beauty and maybe see if we can borrow another vehicle".

"Borrow?" I ask.

"We don't need keys," Joe says. "All we need is the right two ends of the right two wires, and we're good to go".

"You know how to hot-wire a car?" Clyde continues, looking shocked.

Joe smiles. "I know how to do a lot of things, my friend," he says as he slams the hood down at the front of the truck and gives it a reassuring pat. "You know what? It's a fucking waste of time to start trying to fix this damn thing. What we need to do is we need to take a look around, find the fanciest fucking set of wheels in town, and commandeer them so we can get out of here. All those in favor, raise your hands". He holds his hand up, and a moment later Clyde cautiously does the same. "That's two votes in favor," Joe says, smiling at me. "Seems we've got the simple majority we need".

"You can't go around stealing cars," I say, watching as Joe wanders across the road, heading for a small van that's sitting slightly at an angle outside the convenience store.

"Who's gonna stop me?" Joe replies with a grin.

"Yeah, but you can't!" I say again.

"Watch me," Joe says, trying the door but evidently find it locked. "What's the phrase Mom used to use, Thomas? Needs must as the Devil drives? We're in a spot of bother here, and it'd sure do us good to be able to drive off to the next town. If these vehicles are sitting around with no-one using them, why shouldn't we see what we can do?" He stares at me for a moment. "I know your problem," he continues eventually. "You wanna leave things as we found them, just in case everything suddenly gets back to normal. Well, it's not happening, okay? These people aren't coming back. It's survival of the fittest, and I'm definitely one of the fittest".

"Your brother's a confident man," Clyde says quietly to me, looking a little uncomfortable. There's something skittish about this guy, as if he's hiding something. I've been suspicious of him from the start, and this sudden problem with the truck isn't helping.

"You don't know him," I reply.

"He's right, though," Clyde continues. "There's no-one that's gonna come and stop us from taking what we want. You really think a cop's gonna come round the corner and get in our faces?"

"So what do we do?" I ask, turning to Joe. "You want us to just go around looking for trucks to steal?"

"Bingo," Joe replies. "Think of it like you're in a big showroom and you've got a credit card with no limits. There's a few criteria, mind. We need something big, preferably something fairly new. If it looks cool, that's a bonus. Don't worry about whether or not the doors are open or any of that shit. We just need something substantial to get us down the road. You know what I'm saying?"

Shrugging, I turn and start walking along the street. Although I don't like the idea of stealing a truck, I want to get out of Scottsville. Something about the place really freaks me out, and I can't shake the feeling that we might not be alone here for too long. I keep thinking back to that cop who dragged himself to our house, and I keep expecting to see someone similar in the distance.

"Sucks about the truck, huh?" Clyde says as he follows me.

"Yeah," I reply, not wanting to get involved in a conversation right now.

"You know it's not my fault, right?" He keeps pace with me, waiting for me to say something. "I didn't do anything to the truck," he continues eventually. "Not on purpose and not by accident. I swear to God. If you're thinking that this is my fault, it's really not, okay?"

"Okay".

"I just figure, if something odd happens, you're bound to suspect the new guy, especially if he kinda, sorta tried to steal the truck when you first met him. But I swear to God, I want to get out of here as much as you do. More, even. There's a bad energy about Scottsville right now, and I just wanna get somewhere that I can get some answers. You know what I'm saying".

"I don't know if -" I start to say, before suddenly I spot something in a nearby parking lot. "I..." I pause, and my blood runs cold as I realize what we've found.

"I know what you mean," Clyde continues. "I just want some expert to come on the TV and say, like, boom, this is what's going on, and boom, this is how it happened, and boom, this is how we're gonna fix it. You know? I want the fucking facts. It's the not knowing that's the killer". He pauses for a moment. "Kid? You okay?"

I take a deep breath, forcing myself to stay calm.

"Kid?"

"See that white truck?" I say, pointing toward the parking lot.

"Uh, yeah," Clyde replies. "You think that's our wheels?"

"It's my father's truck," I continue. "I've gotta go get my brother," I add, before turning and running back the way we came.

ELIZABETH

Manhattan

WHEN WE REACH THE other side of the bridge, Mallory leads me down to where a bunch of backpacks are piled up against one of the walls, picked out by the moonlight. She crouches down and grabs a pre-packaged sandwich, before adding a number to a piece of paper and then bringing the sandwich over to me.

"Eat," she says.

I open the sandwich to stuff it into my mouth as fast as possible. I feel bad, wolfing down food as soon as I get here, but I'm starving and this is the first thing I've eaten for almost twelve hours. The hunger's so bad, I feel like an animal rooting through a trashcan.

"So I'm guessing this isn't a social call," Mallory says after a moment. "I'll be honest, Elizabeth. I thought it'd be cool if you came, but I wasn't expecting it. What happened?"

"I'm... I just..." I continue eating for a moment. "I got thrown out of the building".

"You got *what*?"

"Bob and Henry," I continue. "They made me leave. They locked the doors and told me they'd never let me back in. I waited and waited, but eventually I realized they were serious, and then I thought I heard a noise down the street and I got scared, and I decided I had to find someone, and you were the only person I could think of, even though you were all the way down here, so I walked and..." My voice trails off as I realize I've just given her something of an info-dump. "Sorry," I add. "I just... things didn't turn out too well".

"So how come you got kicked out?" Mallory asks, leaning back against the wall. "I mean, who the fuck gives anyone the right to kick you out of your own home?"

"It's all some stupid power play thing," I reply, speaking with my mouth full. "My brother's got this weird hero worship deal with Bob".

"I could tell," Mallory says. "When Bob was doing things to me, your brother was just standing by the door and watching. In a way, I thought he was creepier than that Bob guy. I mean, at least with

Bob, I knew what he was doing, but your brother had this look in his eye as if..." She pauses for a moment. "Sorry, he's still your brother. I shouldn't say stuff like that".

"It's fine," I reply, finishing the sandwich. "You're right. There a side of him that I hadn't seen before. It's like he's suddenly become this power-hungry little asshole. I swear to God, the moment Bob put that gun in Henry's hands, everything changed".

"Power corrupts," Mallory replies, with a sad smile on her face. "Bob sounds like a pretty good manipulator. He's a fucking sick bastard, too. If I ever see him again, I swear I'll ram a fucking screwdriver into his face".

"How bad did he hurt you?" I ask cautiously.

She shrugs.

"Pretty bad, huh?"

"There's no point going on about it," she says. "The guy couldn't decide half the time whether he was horny or angry. Sometimes he was both".

"Did he -"

"Let's just keep out of the details," she continues. "Let's just accept that your Bob guy is a bad, bad person". She smiles, but it's a sad smile, as if she's trying to hold back tears. "Let's just leave it at that. If I ever see him again, I'll fucking cut his throat. But I'm not gonna see him again. He's gonna die and rot in this dump, and that's all he deserves".

"But if he hurt you," I say, "you have to do

something".

"Like what? Call the cops?" She laughs, and then she stares at me for a moment. "It doesn't matter," she says eventually. "The past is the past, and we're all more worried about the future right now. You reached us just in time, Elizabeth. We're all packed, ready to leave in the morning".

"Where are you going?"

"We had a group vote. We decided unanimously to get the hell out of this city. It's too dangerous. It's not just about the virus. Think about all those fucking bodies, rotting where they fell. The place is gonna be overrun by disease and rats and stuff. It's gonna be impossible to stay here, so we're gonna stick together and head west. Kendricks figures there has to be some workable land out there, and if we can reach the Great Lakes, we might be able to do some serious fishing". She shrugs. "It seems kind of crazy, planning to walk so far, but we haven't really got much choice. I don't know how long it's gonna take, but the journey's worth making". She stares at me. "You can come, if you want".

"Me?"

"Why not? You're healthy, aren't you?"

"Yeah, but -"

"How long are you gonna wait?" she asks, interrupting me.

"For what?"

"For your brother. Are you gonna wait 'til it's almost too late? Longer? Are you just gonna stick it out in New York forever, hoping he'll realize he's being an ass? Are you gonna wait and wait until you end up dying?"

"I'll be okay," I say, glancing over at the pitch-black park and realizing that I really might end up sitting here alone tomorrow. The city's already creepy, and I genuinely don't know what I'd do if I was left alone. I know that everything Mallory is saying is technically correct, and the logical choice would be to join these people and leave. I mean, it's pretty clear that my parents aren't coming back. At the same time, there's no way I can leave Henry behind; despite everything he's done and said over the past couple of days, he's still my flesh and blood, and he's the only family left in my life. I should leave, but I won't.

"I'm gonna be blunt with you," Mallory continues. "I get why you'd think you have to stay here and keep track of your brother. But at the same time, this fucking city is gonna become a hellhole real fast, and if you stay here, you're gonna die. Not just you, but him too. So you've got to leave at some point. Why not now? I mean, all that brother shit and the family tie stuff, that's from the old world. It doesn't count anymore. It's every man for himself".

"He's my brother," I remind her.

"And you're his sister," she says, "but that

doesn't give either of you the right to force the other one to do something that's gonna get you killed". She pauses for a moment. "What about your parents?"

"What about them?"

"You still waiting for them to show up?"

I sigh. "No," I say eventually, feeling a strange tightening sensation in my chest. The truth is, I realized as I walked here tonight that I have to stop hoping that my parents are going to come back, but it still feels strange to say the words out loud. "They're not coming," I continue after a moment. I can feel tears behind my eyes, but something's preventing me from crying.

"You think they're dead?" Mallory asks.

I nod.

"Mine too. Hopefully, anyway". She smiles. "I had a bad relationship with them. But the point is, if you can accept that your parents aren't around anymore, why can't you just do the same thing with your brother?"

I shake my head. "You really don't get it, do you? He's family".

"So what?"

"So I can't just abandon him".

"Even if it means that you'll die?" She pauses. "Even if it means that you'll let him keep you here when you know it's a mistake? Are you really willing to follow him straight into your grave,

Elizabeth?"

"I just..." I take a deep breath, and I realize that there's no way I can explain my decision. It's just that on an emotional level, I can't bring myself to abandon Henry. I still feel like there's some way I can get him away from Bob and make him see sense. I just can't do it in time for us to leave with Mallory and the others.

"It's suicide," Mallory says after a moment. "You know that, right? If you come with us, you'll be with people who have a plan. It's a long shot, but I think we've actually got a chance of making it work. If you stay here, you're basically killing yourself. I mean, what are you gonna do? Are you gonna just sit around outside your building, hoping that one day they'll let you back in? Isn't that kind of pathetic?"

I nod. She's right. Everything she's saying is right, and I can't argue at all. Looking over at the dark buildings that rise up from the street, I realize that by staying in the city for Henry, I'm making it almost certain that I'll die. But I can't leave. Not without Henry.

THOMAS

Oklahoma

THE THREE OF US stand in the parking lot, staring at the truck. It's been five days since my father packed up some stuff and drove off to Scottsville, promising he'd be back within twenty-four hours. He never came back, of course, and after waiting a few days, we started to accept that he'd got caught up in whatever was happening. By the time we reached Scottsville ourselves, I'd given up any hope that we might find him, and now suddenly he's here. Or rather, his truck's here, parked up ominously by the side of the diner.

One thing's for sure: whatever prevented him from coming home, it must have been something big. He was the kind of guy who usually stayed well out of trouble, and it's hard to believe that he'd have allowed himself to get mixed up in anything dangerous. I don't get why he wouldn't have just turned around and headed straight home as soon as he saw that there was trouble in Scottsville, although he had a tendency to be a little nosy. He probably parked up and thought he could help out, and then he got busy and suddenly it was too late to get away.

"He said he was coming to the diner," Joe says eventually, a hint of fear in his voice. "It's almost the last thing I remember him saying. He said he was gonna come here and..." His voices trails off.

"This is where he always came when he was in Scottsville," I reply, keeping my eyes fixed on the truck. I remember the days when he used to bring me along for the ride, and we'd end up sitting in the diner for hours. My father was the kind of guy who could walk into pretty much any room and always find someone he knew; I'd sit and listen to him chatting on and on to whoever else he happened to run into. It used to get pretty boring, most of the time, and I'd stare out the window and wish I could be somewhere else. Those days seem so long ago now, even though the last time was probably just a couple of months back.

"At least we know he made it, then," Joe says.

We stand in silence a little longer. I know I sure as hell don't wanna go and look in the truck, or look in the diner, and I'm guessing Joe feels the same way. I mean, the odds are that our father's either in the truck or in the diner, and either way he's probably not in the best shape. Then again, we need to know what happened, and we can't stand here like gawking idiots forever. At some point, one of us is gonna have to go and take a look.

"You see that?" Clyde asks, pointing over at the diner.

Squinting, I finally spot what he means: there's a figure in the diner, slumped in a booth by the window. With a thick shock of white hair, he's clearly not my father, but he's proof that people are dying around here. There's just something about the way his head is resting against the glass, as if he's exhausted.

"That's not him," I say after a moment.

"Just some old fuck," Joe adds, as if he feels the need to make some kind of obnoxious comment whenever he gets the opportunity.

"This whole place is fucked," I say quietly, under my breath.

"He's probably in the truck," Joe says coldly.

"You want me to go take a look?" Clyde asks.

"No," Joe says, swallowing hard. "No, I'm gonna do it". He takes a deep breath, psyching himself up for the moment. "Thomas," he says after a moment. "You've gotta wait here, okay? Just... wait right here". He starts walking slowly toward the truck, taking a kind of circular path that leads him around the vehicle, as if he's checking that there's nothing hiding anywhere. It's almost as if he expects something to jump out from the other side.

"Are you sure it's your Dad's truck?" Clyde whispers to me.

I nod.

"He's probably fine," he continues. "He probably just left it to..." His voice trails off, and thankfully he keeps quiet as we watch Joe getting closer to the driver's side window. Eventually, he peers in through the glass, and then he just kind of stands there for a while, not saying anything. He's obviously seen something.

"Do you think he's found anything?" Clyde whispers.

I turn and shoot him a dark, angry look.

"I was just wondering," he replies, looking down at the ground.

"He's here," Joe says simply.

"What?" I call out to him.

He clears his throat. "I said, he's here. What are you, fucking deaf?"

I pause, my heart pounding in my chest. "What do you mean?" I ask.

"I mean he's here. In the truck. Down on the

seats. It's him".

I close my eyes for a moment. "How is he?"

Silence.

Opening my eyes, I see that Joe hasn't moved. He's still just standing there, staring into the truck as if he can't quite believe what he's seeing. "Joe?" I call out. He still doesn't reply, and I start walking over to join him.

"Don't come any closer!" Joe calls out to me.

I stop in my tracks. "What do you see?" I ask, even though I'm pretty sure I can guess. It takes a lot to make Joe go so quiet, and right now there's only one thing that could do the job.

"He's in there," he replies."He's, kind of, slumped over, and he's..." He pauses for a moment. "The sickness," he continues after a moment. "How's that look again?"

I take a deep breath. "Like, kind of, yellow and gray skin," I tell him. "And I think... like, a swollen belly sometimes, stuff like that. And blood and pus, coughed up and..." I pause, thinking back to how Lydia looked when I found her body, and how my mother looked when I found her sitting in the kitchen yesterday morning, and the cop. A shiver passes through my body as I realize that already, in just a week, I've seen three dead people. I really don't wanna add a fourth to that list.

"Seems about right," Joe says.

"Is that what he looks like?"

He nods.

I pause for a moment, as this sensation of dread starts to creep through my body. "Is he..." I pause again, feeling stupid for even asking the question. "Is he... I mean, does he look like he's moving at all?"

Joe turns to me with a scowl on his face. "Moving?"

"Like..." I take a deep breath. "Forget it".

"He's dead," he replies. "So, no. He's not moving".

We all stand in silence for a moment, as if none of us has any idea what to do. Joe seems to be just staring through the window of the truck, transfixed by the sight of our father's dead body; although there's a part of me that wants to go over and join him, and look inside to see how things ended up, I can't bring myself to take the handful of steps that would be necessary. I feel like I'm rooted to the spot, struggling to come to terms with the fact that both our parents are now dead. Strangely, after a moment, I start wondering whether this means Joe and I are orphans now. I mean, is there a cut-off point where you're too old to be considered an orphan? For some reason, it's this bizarre procedural question that preoccupies me, as if this is a way to avoid having a more emotional response.

"Let's do this," Joe says suddenly, walking around to the back of the truck.

"Do what?" I ask, shocked by his sudden burst of movement.

"This," he says, grabbing a couple of cans of gasoline. Before I can say anything, he's already opened one of the cans, and he's started dousing the truck. I watch in stunned silence as he covers the entire vehicle, and then he walks over to the side of the parking lot and grabs a small rock.

"Joe?" I ask, as he heads back to the truck.

"Busy," he replies, before using the rock to smash the side window. "Jesus!" he shouts, stepping back.

"What?"

"Fucking stinks," he says, before opening the other gasoline can and pouring its contents through the broken window.

"Joe -" I start to say.

"You got matches?" he asks.

"No, but do you think -"

"We need to burn this fucker," he continues, ignoring me. "We need to fucking incinerate the whole damn thing until it's just a pile of ash".

"I have this," Clyde says, pulling a small cigarette lighter from his pocket. "It's not much, but it -"

"It'll do," Joe says, holding out a hand. "Send it over here".

Clyde throws the lighter, and we watch as Joe flicks it open and gets a small flame burning.

181

He takes off his jacket and then removes his shirt, which he lights and holds close to the truck. "Anyone got anything they wanna say?" he asks. "Thought not". With that, he throws the shirt through the window and steps back as gasoline immediately ignites, quickly covering the entire truck with flames.

"Like a Viking burial," Clyde says, as the heat from the fire reaches us.

"Like a what?" I ask, turning to him.

"Like a Viking burial," he continues. "This is what the Vikings did".

I stare at him for a moment. "The Vikings burned people in trucks in parking lots?"

"No," he says, "but they put their dead on rafts and sent them out to sea, with fires burning so that eventually the raft would burn up and sink".

"That's nothing like this," Joe says, sound a little contemptuous of the whole idea. "Come on," he adds, "we should get going. There might be a load of gas in the tank. It'd be a fucking stupid way to die if the thing explodes and takes us out".

Turning and walking away, we get as far as the street corner before there's a huge explosion behind us. Turning, I see that the truck has been completely destroyed, and all that's left now is a roaring fire that's sending thick black smoke up into the sky. It's hard to believe that our father's dead body is in there, and that we've now burned both our parents in the space of little more than twenty-four hours.

"I'm sure he didn't suffer," Clyde says.

"Of course he fucking suffered," Joe spits back at him. "The guy died in his truck, probably coughing his guts up. Probably a pretty painful way to go, if you ask me". With that, he turns and starts walking away. "Let's get moving, people!" he calls back to us. "We still need to find ourselves a vehicle so we can get out of this shit-hole!"

"Your brother's an interesting guy," Clyde says, turning to me.

"That's one way of putting it," I reply.

"I'm sorry about you father".

I shrug.

"If you want to talk about it -"

"Why would I wanna talk about it?" I ask. "Joe's right. We've gotta get on with finding a truck or something, so we can get moving. This isn't a good place to be". In order to avoid having this conversation drag on any longer, I turn and start walking toward the main street, and after a moment I hear Clyde's footsteps following me. By the time we get to the main street, I can't hear the fire from the parking lot; glancing back, though, I can still see the smoke as it rises into the sky. For a moment, I feel like I want to mark the moment in some way, but then I realize that there's no point. He's dead, and that's all there is to it. Anything else would be a waste of time.

ELIZABETH

Manhattan

"YOU'VE GOT ONE HOUR to change your mind," Mallory says as she walks past me, carrying one of the backpacks.

It's almost midday, and for the past few hours I've been watching as the others prepare for their journey. They seem to have it all figured out: their provisions are packed away neatly, and they've even managed to get a map from a nearby bookstore. They're organized and efficient, and I feel like a total spare wheel, wandering around behind Mallory, offering to help but generally being rebuffed. I should have left at sunrise, but the thought of being left alone again is too much to handle.

"Having second thoughts?" Kendricks asks as he studies the map.

"No," I reply quickly.

"Then you're even more insane than I thought".

I turn to him.

"You know what I mean," he continues with a smile. "Think about it, Elizabeth. In less than half an hour, we're all gonna start walking out of here, and we're not gonna stop until we get to this spot just north of Chicago". He points to a location on the map. "It's crazy, and it's dangerous, but it's less crazy and less dangerous than just sitting around".

"I know," I say firmly, feeling as if I'm about to get the same lecture I was given by Mallory last night.

"I have a wife," Kendricks says. "We've been married three years. Her name's Debra and she's a teacher over on the west side. She's pregnant, actually. Three months gone. We were gonna let our friends and family know this week, but..." He pauses for a moment. "Last week, she flew to Miami to see her parents and tell them. I was gonna go, but at the last minute work kept me behind. I love her, and I miss her, but I know she's not coming back".

"You don't *know* that," I say.

He nods. "I do. I really do. The odds of her surviving are almost a million to one, and then the odds of her making it here are even lower, and the odds of me finding her in Miami are tiny. I just keep telling myself that she wouldn't want me to sit around in New York and wait for her while the rats get bigger and the whole fucking place becomes a disease-ridden cess-pit".

"Then why don't you go to Miami and look for her?" I ask.

"Because it'd take years, and because Miami's not gonna be much better than New York in the long-run". He pauses. "To be honest, Elizabeth, I've surprised myself. I've managed to be kinda logical and hard-hearted about the whole thing. I keep thinking I should be irrational, but it's just not in my nature. I'm accepting the situation as it is, and I'm moving on. Does that make me a bad husband? In normal circumstances, yes. But these aren't normal circumstances. We have to do what we can, and I don't believe that any of us has a duty to die just because we feel this need to demonstrate our loyalty to someone else. Do I sound like an asshole?"

I stare at him. "A little," I say eventually. "And logical".

He smiles sadly. "You know the worst thing? I know you're right. But the world has changed, and we have to change with it. Family ties from the old world are irrelevant now. I could head on down to Miami on some crazy junket to find my wife, but do you know what'd happen? I'd die. It's as simple as that. All I can do is try to survive, and try to rebuild, and hope that she's doing the same thing. If you're smart, you'll do the same thing with your brother. He's old enough to make his own decisions. If he wants to stick around in New York with some power-mad nut-job, let him. I just hate to think of you in a couple of weeks, dying on the street while your brother's dying in that building".

"I can't leave," I say.

"He's just your brother," Mallory continues, wandering back over to join us. "Not even a good one, either. He seems like an asshole. I know I shouldn't say that, but it's true. There's a darkness in his eyes, Elizabeth. Maybe you don't see it 'cause you're too close to him, but the way he looked at me while Bob was... You know what I mean. Most people wouldn't be so easily led. There's something wrong with Henry. He's not right in the head, and I don't think you can continue to treat him like he's a normal person. It's not worth dying for him".

"Come on," says one of the others. "We're already late setting off".

"Goodbye, Elizabeth," Kendricks says, coming over and shaking my hand as the others start walking away. "We're going to hopefully be somewhere on the south-eastern shore of Lake Ontario. If something happens and you end up leaving New York, please consider coming out to find us. With any luck, we'll be able to get ourselves set up pretty fast. The journey should take about a month, but we're gonna be able to go to Rochester for supplies. That's the plan, anyway. I know it's as hell of a long-shot, but you'll be welcome". With that, he smiles and walks away, following the others across the park.

"I'll be there in a minute!" Mallory calls after him, before taking my hands in hers. "Elizabeth," she says, adopting a serious tone, "I know we've only known each other for a couple of days, but I guess in this type of situation, you kind of form bonds pretty fast. I really just hate to see you throwing your life away like this. You've got an opportunity to get the hell out of here, and you're pissing it away just 'cause you think you can save your brother. You can't. He's made his choice, and you're letting him drag you down too. Do you really think your parents would want you to do this? They'd want at least *one* of their kids to make the right choice, wouldn't they?"

I nod, but I can't say anything. A tear rolls down my cheek, and my bottom lip is trembling.

"You can't be a hero," she continues. "You can't sacrifice yourself like some kind of martyr, just because you think you've got a duty to save your brother. He's old enough to make his own decisions, and so are you. You've gotta let him go sometime, so why not now?"

"I need to help him," I say, my voice trembling as I try to stop crying.

"You can't," she replies. "So why not be the one who does the smart thing? Let Henry do what he wants. Let him sit around with that Bob guy. You need to do what's best for your own life, Elizabeth. You can't just follow him around. His head's not right. If he really, truly thinks he's better off staying here with that fucking asshole Bob, then there's nothing you can do to change his mind. Just wish him luck and head on out of town".

I nod again, feeling as if I can't actually get any words out.

"Come here," she says, stepping closer and giving me a strong hug. "I wish I could change your mind," she says quietly, her mouth just a couple of inches from my ear. "I wish I could drug you or something, or go and get your brother and drag him along with us. I wish I could go to that building, find Bob and smash his fucking face in. Seriously, nothing would give me greater please than to take a baseball bat to that fucker's face. Are you sure there's nothing I can do or say to make you realize that you should -"

"I guess this is goodbye, then," she says eventually, stepping back a couple of paces. "Remember where we are, okay? The south-eastern shore of Lake Ontario. Somewhere around there, anyway. It might take a bit of time for us to find a good plot of land, but we'll manage it eventually, and then... Well, you know what I mean, right? We're gonna find a way to grow our own food, and we're gonna start all over again. It'll be like when people first came to America all those years ago. If there's any chance you can make it out there to join us, any chance at all -"

"I'll get Henry," I say, taking a deep breath in an attempt to hold back the tears, "and then maybe we'll come after you some day".

"Okay," she replies, with tears in her eyes. I can tell she doesn't believe for a second that she'll ever see me again. This feels like a permanent goodbye, even if neither of us can quite admit the truth.

"Just go!" I say firmly, forcing myself to smile. "Go! You're gonna get left behind if you wait much longer!"

She turns and walks away, hurrying across the park until she's caught up with the others.

I stand and watch as they leave. After a few minutes, they're just little dots in the distance, and finally they disappear one by one through a gate and out the park. Once they're out of sight, I turn and look around at the emptiness. Sure, there are probably a few people still alive, scattered in the city, but I know I've just turned down my last and best hope to get out of here. There's a part of me that wants to run after Mallory, Kendricks and the rest, and take up their offer, but I know I can't leave Henry behind. He's my brother, and I'm going to stay here until I can make him see reason. He's not an idiot; I'm convinced I can show him the truth, if I can just get him to see past Bob. Whatever else happens, I have to stick close to my family, because Henry's all I've got.

Turning, I make my way back across the park. I feel as if I have to go back and talk to Henry. I've just put my life on the line for him; if he doesn't come through for me in return, I'm dead.

THOMAS

Oklahoma

"FUCK!" JOE SHOUTS, as the spanner slips and slices a small cut on the side of his thumb. "Fuck!" He steps back before aiming a hard kick at the side of the truck. "Fucking thing!"

It's been a couple of hours now since we burned our father's truck. We spent a while looking for another vehicle, but no-one in Scottsville seems to have owned anything much bigger than a pick-up, so Joe's decided he's gonna have another try at fixing whatever's wrong with our original truck. To that end, he's spent the past half-hour tinkering with things under the hood and getting increasingly annoyed. For a guy who's always claimed to be good with engines, he seems to be coming up blank right now.

"You okay?" I ask, sitting in the doorway of Clyde's house.

"Yeah," Joe mutters. "I'm fine. I had too much blood anyway". He sucks at the cut on his finger. "Fuck this," he says eventually, hurrying around to the back of the truck and grabbing a jack. He comes over to my side, sticks the jack under one of the front wheels, and starts pumping it up.

"*Now* what are you doing?" I ask. It's hard to escape the conclusion that Joe's running out of ideas, and he seems to be randomly and angrily attacking the truck from all angles, as if he's hoping to fix the problem my accident.

"Fixing the fucking truck," he spits back at me. "What does it look like I'm doing?" He keeps pumping the jack, until finally he's got the front part of the truck a few inches off the ground. "That oughta do it," he says. "Tommy boy, you're gonna have to pass me stuff as I ask for it, okay? I'm gonna get this fucker sorted, if it's the last thing I fucking do". With that, he gets down onto the ground and wriggles under the truck, until all I can see of him is his legs poking out the side. "Spanner!" he barks.

Getting up and wandering over to where the tools are laid out, I grab the spanner and take it over to him. He snatches it from my hand and carries on working, leaving me to just stand there and wait for my next order. I swear, sometimes Joe treats me like I'm just a slave. It wouldn't be so bad if he could actually fix the damn truck, but I can't help feeling that he's just gonna spend all day tinkering and then he'll give up and get pissed off. We're still gonna end up stealing a new vehicle, so this whole 'fixing' charade seems like a total waste of time. If our father was here, he'd know how to sort it all out...

"Wrench," Joe calls out.

"What?"

"Wrench!" He sighs. "You paying attention up there, or is it time for your daily jerk-off?"

"Fine," I reply, turning and walking away.

"Hey, where are you going?" he shouts.

"To look for something," I say, making my way quickly along the street.

"What?" he shouts.

"Fuck you," I mutter under my breath.

"Get your fucking ass back here!" he yells. "Thomas! Where the fuck do you think you're going?"

Ignoring him, I turn and head into the next street. There's something about Joe that's driving me crazy right now. I can't stand the way he thinks he can spend days and days drinking and being nothing more than a drunk dick, and then suddenly he thinks he's in charge of everything. I swear to God, if he could actually fix the truck, I'd be willing to put up with his crap, but I know damn well that he's not gonna get the thing working, even if he spends the rest of his life fiddling around under there. Still, he acts like he's our fucking savior and like everyone's supposed to be grateful for his *amazing* skills.

Reaching another intersection, I turn and look along the deserted streets. I swear to God, Scottsville is the most depressing town in the world. Even when there were people here, it was bad enough. Now that it's a creepy, empty wasteland, it's worse than ever. Part of me wants to smash own a load of doors and see if there's a load of corpses piled up in the buildings, but I figure the best thing to do is just to hope we get out of here as soon as possible. I can't stop thinking about that cop I saw back at our farm; Joe doesn't take it seriously, but I keep thinking the cop was a sign that there's something seriously fucked up going on here. What if there are other 'things' like the cop? What if -

Suddenly I hear the loudest, most agonized scream I've ever heard in my life. I stop dead in my tracks as the scream continues, and after a moment I realize it's coming from near Clyde's house. I turn and race back around the corner, and I immediately see what's happened: the jack seems to have slipped out from under the truck, and the vehicle has come thumping down straight onto Joe. He's yelling for help, and as I race over to him, I can already see a pool of blood seeping out across the ground.

Whatever's happened, it's bad.

"Joe!" I shout as I scramble down onto my hands and knees next to him. The wheel of the truck has crunched into the side of his chest, and I can see a sharp piece of bone sticking out from his ribcage. For a moment, I'm completely frozen with fear and I can't work out what to do. Seconds later, I hear movement over by the door.

"What the hell happened?" Clyde shouts as he runs over to us.

"I think the jack slipped," I say, as Joe continues to scream.

"We need to get it back up," Clyde says, grabbing the jack and shoving one end back under the wheel. "This is gonna hurt, but it's the only way". He starts pumping it up, and Joe lets out a gurgled cry of pain as the wheel slowly moves up to reveal that the right side of his chest has been crushed. There's blood pouring out from the wound, and several pieces of fractured and broken bone are jutting out from beneath the flesh. The whole side of his upper torso looks like a mess, and there's damage to his shoulder and the top of his arm.

"What the fuck?" I say, feeling a cold chill rush through my body. It's as if my skin just tightened, and I can feel my heart pounding in my chest. "What do we do?" I shout, turning to Clyde. "What the hell do we do?"

"We, uh..." he says, his eyes wide open with

shock. "We... We get him inside," he splutters, clearly making it up as he goes along.

At that moment, Joe lets out another scream, and this time blood erupts from his mouth.

"I've got a first aid kit," Clyde says.

"We need more than that," I say. "How are we gonna move him?"

Clyde shakes his head.

"If we pick him up, we might make it worse," I continue, starting to really panic. "Look at his arm! It might fall off!"

"We can't just leave him here!" Clyde shouts back at me. "His arm won't fall of. We need to stabilize him and clean this shit up!" He pauses for a moment. "I'll take the legs, you take his shoulders. It's the only way". He stares at me. "Thomas, if we leave him here like this, he's gonna die!"

Shuffling around, I reach under the truck and do my best to support Joe's shoulders as Clyde grabs hold of his feet.

"It's gonna be okay," I say, looking down at my brother's face and seeing his features contorted by pain. "It's gonna be okay," I say again, even though I'm not sure that there's anything we can do to help him.

"Okay," Clyde says. "You ready? Three. Two. One". He starts pulling, and Joe screams as we ease him out from under the truck. I've never heard a human being scream so loud, not even in movies.

Grabbing Joe's shoulders, I lift him up and we carry him up the steps and into Clyde's house. Blood drips down from the wound as we hurry over to the kitchen table, which Clyde brushes clear before we carefully set Joe down. More blood is flowing from his wound, and Clyde quickly grabs a towel and holds it against the wound. It seems so futile and pointless, and I can't shake the thought that there's no way we can do anything to fix this.

"Now what?" I shout.

Clyde shakes his head. "We have to stop the bleeding," he says, "but I don't know how. We have to make him clot somehow. He's already lost too much blood".

"How do we stop it?" I shout.

"Hold this," he says. "Hold the towel firmly against the wound. Really hard, okay? Don't worry about hurting him. Hurting him's good. At least if he's hurting, he's alive. I think we just have to keep the hole plugged until the bleeding stops".

As I take the towel and apply pressure to the injury, Joe lets out another scream of pain. There's blood dribbling down from the corner of his lips, and he seems to be struggling a little less, as if he's losing consciousness. I can feel ragged, splintered bone on the other side of the towel.

"I can't stop the bleeding," I say, as blood soaks through the towel and onto my hands.

Looking over at Joe's face, I see that his eyes have closed. "Joe! Wake up!" I shout, but his eyes barely even flicker. With blood pooling all over the floor, I'm starting to think it's too late to save him. The towel is now completely soaked, and blood continues to pour out every second. "Joe!" I shout, desperate to keep him awake. "Joe!"

ELIZABETH

Manhattan

FIFTH AVENUE IS DESERTED. So are Madison Avenue, East 59th Street and the whole of Midtown. The whole city. I don't know why, but I can't shake the hope that maybe this is going to turn out to be a dream; I keep thinking that I'll turn a corner and suddenly all the noise and light and craziness of New York will be switched back on, as if it's never been away. No matter how many times I tell myself that this is all real, I just can't seem to let go of that thin, fragile hope.

The evidence in front of my eyes, however, is brutal. The city is dead and bare. It's as if no-one has ever been here, even though it's only a week since I was walking these streets and struggling to get through the huge crowds. There's nothing around but an ominous, oppressive silence that makes my footsteps seem louder than ever.

As I make my way through the Bowery, I spot something in the distance. At first, I think it's just a pile of garbage, but as I get closer I realize that it's a bunch of rats, massing in a doorway. I make sure to give them a wide berth, even though they seem to be totally focused on whatever they're doing. After a moment, some of the rats move down to the ground and I see the skeletal face of a person, its bones picked clean by the rats. I stop for a moment, stunned by the sight. I should probably run, but this whole thing is starting to feel like such a nightmare, it's almost as if I'm trapped in some kind of trance. I stare and stare at the dead face and -

Feeling a sudden pain around my left ankle, I step back and look down to see a rat scurrying between my feet. Just as I start to wonder whether he bit me, he attacks my other ankle, tearing off a piece of flesh. I turn and run down the middle of the street, until finally I get to the next intersection and I look back to see that the rats have all returned to the dead body. Looking across the street, I see the entrance to a subway station, with more rats scurrying in and out; they're probably feeding on the bodies down below. Suddenly, I start to panic about the rat bite, in case it might have infected me.

Sitting down, I spit on the injury and try to wipe it clean; eventually, I hold my ankle up and start sucking on the wound, hoping that I can clean it before it becomes too serious. Finally, I give up and take a deep breath, staring along the empty street and realizing that Mallory and Kendricks were right: the rats are going to take over soon.

Hauling myself back up, I continue my journey back to the building. It's far too late to consider changing my mind, and I know I could never have *actually* left Henry behind. For better or worse, I've made my decision and now I have to see if I can find some way to make this work. It's not impossible that I might be able to talk Henry around and make him see the truth about Bob's influence. Together, we can still strike out from New York and make our way somewhere new. I might even be able to get him to come with me to Lake Ontario, and we can find the others. It sounds crazy, and the odds are slim, but at least it's something that *might* work. With all the rats starting to show up on the streets of New York, it's a better idea than just doing nothing.

"Hey!" says a voice nearby.

Almost jumping out of my skin, I turn to see a man coming toward me from a nearby intersection. He looks to be quite a bit older than me, maybe in his forties or even his fifties, and he's wearing a shabby-looking business suit with no shoes. To be honest, he's the kind of guy I'd usually cross the street to avoid, but in a situation like this I guess that's not really an option.

"What do you want?" I ask, starting to back away.

"Nothing," he says, smiling. "I just saw you and thought I'd say hello".

"I don't have anything," I continue, backing away a little further. "If you want food -"

"I don't want food," he replies. "I don't *want* anything. Honestly, I was just passing and I saw you, so I figured I'd say hello. It's been a while since I saw a friendly face. I've been walking nearly two days non-stop, and you're the first alive person I've run into".

I stare at him. To be honest, I want to just get away from his as fast as possible, but at the same time he seems friendly enough and I don't feel like I have the energy to run. There's even a part of me that worries I might have started hallucinating; maybe I'm just standing here alone, talking to thin air?

"You're scared," he says after a moment. "That's okay. I understand. I'm scared too. Only a fucking madman wouldn't be scared at a time like this. Planes falling from the sky, dead bodies piling up. Everything's so calm and quiet. I've been walking around for a couple of days, and I swear to God, this place is fucking creepy. I mean, it was creepy before, but now it's off the scale, you know what I mean?" He turns and looks into the distance. "There's supposed to be people in a place like this," he says eventually. "New York's supposed to be full to the brim with people bustling and hurrying all over the place, but..." He glances back at me. "I just saw *some* people. A bunch of them, heading over the bridge. Looked like they were heading out of town. Maybe they're the smart ones. I think I'm gonna get out of here myself. I guess I should have run and caught them and maybe gone their way, but I waited too long and now it's too late. Still, I've got legs. I can get out under my own steam. Too many rats around these parts for my liking. I fucking hate rats".

"Me too," I reply, looking over at a nearby doorway and seeing a couple of rats scurrying along the sidewalk. "They're everywhere".

"I don't blame them," the guy says. "If I was a rat, I'd be doing the same thing. This is perfect for them, if you think about it. New York's always been full of garbage, but now they don't even have to contend with humans. I swear, this is gonna be a city of rats before too long. I wouldn't be surprised if they start organizing into little communities, walking on their back legs, and chatting shit". He smiles. "That's a joke, but stranger things have happened. Speaking of which, have you been down into the subway lately?"

I shake my head.

"Don't," he replies. "Just... don't. That's my advice to you. It's not nice down there, There's a lot of dead folk, all piled up everywhere. The rats have found them, of course. Some of those little bastards are getting so big and fat, I started to think they could take *me* down". He smiles. "My name's George Crow. Do you mind if I ask *your* name?"

"Elizabeth," I tell him. "Elizabeth Marter".

"Elizabeth, huh?" He laughs. "From the Hebrew, meaning God's daughter or God's promise. Nice name. Not as nice as George Crow, but nice enough. George is a Greek name, referring to a farmer". He pauses. "You've gotta pay attention to names, Elizabeth Marter. They have meanings. It might just seem like a superstition, but there's more to it. A person grows into their name, whether they like it or not".

I smile politely, figuring that this guy is perhaps a little crazy in the head.

"Well, Elizabeth Marter, daughter of God," he says after a moment, "I think I'm gonna get on my way. I've got a long way to go, even if I don't entirely know the right direction, but I'd like to leave something with you, if that's okay?" He reaches into his blazer pocket and pulls out a black feather, which he holds out to me. "Take it," he continues. "It's for you". He waits for me to say something. "Go on, take it".

"Why?" I ask.

"Why not?"

"I don't..." I stare at the feather, and I can't shake the feeling that it's something I shouldn't accept. In fact, the more I look at it, the more I feel as if something terrible would happen if I even touched the damn thing. "I don't want it," I tell him eventually.

"It's just a feather".

"Thanks, but... It's yours. You keep it".

He sighs, before putting the feather back into his pocket. "Well," he says, clearly a little put out by my refusal to take the gift. "I know better than to argue with a lady. You don't want the feather, you don't want the feather. I'll just hang onto it, in case it's needed some other time. I hope you manage to get by, Elizabeth Marter. If you want my advice, don't stay in the city too long. Get out of here. Head somewhere else. Sooner rather than later, those rats are gonna get so big, they'll be able to bust down doors". He turns and starts walking away. "Maybe you should head west," he calls back to me. "You never know, you might meet someone interesting! A lot of good things have come out of folks heading west!"

I watch as he walks away. There something slightly creepy about that guy; he had an expression that made me feel as if he thought he was somehow better than me, or that he thought he knew something special. With my heart racing, I stand and watch until he disappears into the distance, and then I turn and carry on walking back toward my building. There was something pretty weird about the way that guy tried to give me a feather, but I guess there are some pretty weird people around. As I walk, I keep glancing over my shoulder; I almost expect to find George Crow following me, but he's nowhere to be seen. I guess he and his feather have got somewhere else to be.

Eventually I reach the street where I live, and I spot my building a few hundred feet away. I make my way carefully to the corner, and finally I glance through the front window and into the lobby. Sure enough, I spot Henry, sitting at his post with his rifle slung over his shoulder. He looks as if he's taking is guard role very seriously, and it's almost like he doesn't care that I've gone. I guess, to him, I'm still a traitor thanks to my decision to help Mallory get away. I wish I could run through the door and shake him until he comes to his senses, but I know that wouldn't work. I need to be smarter and more careful, so I hurry around the back of the building and manage to slip through into the yard that links the service entrance to the rear of the nearby hotel.

Although I still don't have a plan, I know I can't just hang about in the city and wait for an idea to pop into my head. I figure I'll come up with something, eventually; all I need to do is get to Henry and talk to him when Bob's not around. He's my brother, after all, so I'm certain I can find a way to make him see reason. Making my way quickly across the yard, I try the back door, but it's locked. The same goes for all the windows, and I suddenly realize that even the first step - getting inside the building - is going to be difficult. Stepping back, I look up at the windows on the side of the building, and I see that they're all closed. I try to think of some other way in, of some route that Henry and Bob might not have remembered, but I can't think of anything. Frankly, I'm not sure how -

Suddenly a hand grabs my face, pulling me back as another hand grips me firmly around the waist.

"What a surprise," Bob hisses into my ear. "You came slinking back, just like a rat". I feel a jolt deep in the base of my neck, and everything goes black.

THOMAS

Oklahoma

"AT LEAST THE BLEEDING'S STOPPED,"
Clyde says, as he wipes his hands clean. "I don't
know how much he lost, but..." He glances back
over at Joe, who's unconscious on the kitchen table.
"The fact that the blood's stopped means that his
body's started to heal. I guess that means he's
fighting back, and he's stable. That's something".

"Stable's good, right?" I say. "Stable means
he's gonna get better?"

"I guess it means he's not getting worse," he
replies. "I don't know. He lost a *lot* of blood. A hell
of a lot. I don't know how the body recovers from
something like that. And the wound... He needs
proper medical attention. Anything we do for him is

just patching him up. We need to get him to a doctor. I mean, only a doctor can really work out what the hell needs to be done with an injury like that. If you look at how big it is, I reckon one of his lungs has to have been damaged".

"Then we've got to find people," I say. "We need to get him to somewhere where there's lots of people. We need to go to a city".

"Tulsa's closest," Clyde says. "I guess it's more likely that we'll find a doctor there than anywhere. One thing's for certain, though. There's no way we can just stick him back together and expect him to recover. The guy's gonna get an infection. You saw the size of that wound, and to be honest, the towel wasn't exactly sterile. Nothing about this whole place is sterile. I wouldn't even want to clean a paper-cut on that table".

I look down at Joe's bloodied torso. "If we don't try to help him," I say quietly, "he'll die".

"There's gotta be a truck," Clyde says. "Somewhere in this whole town, there has *got* to be a truck tucked away somewhere. I saw people with trucks. There was a guy who used to transport stuff between towns, and there was a guy who had a couple of fields nearby. You can't tell me that they don't have trucks. We just need to get better at looking. We need to go through garages and gardens until we find something, and then we need to get them started".

"Joe was the one who knew how to hot-wire the ignition," I point out.

"Then we'll practice on other vehicles," he continues. "We can't sit around waiting for someone else to help us. We need to get on with it, and if that means learning a few new tricks, then I guess that's just what we'll have to do. You can't seriously think that it's beyond the pair of us to steal a fucking truck from somewhere".

I nod, realizing he's right.

"You know..." He pauses, as if he's reluctant to get the words out. "I don't mean to be down on things, and I don't mean to scare you, but I think you need to prepare yourself for the possibility that not everything is gonna work out".

I stare at him for a moment. "What do you mean?"

"I mean... We're gonna try to get your brother to some place where he can get helped, but the odds of that working are... You know what I mean, right?"

"No," I say firmly, "I don't know what you mean. Why don't you come out and say it?"

He sighs. "Just accept that the odds are stacked against us, okay? He's lost a lot of blood, and an injury like that would be difficult to fix at the best of times -"

"He's gonna make it!" I say, raising my voice a little.

"But if he doesn't," Clyde continues. "I mean, like I said, he's lost so much blood, and that's not good. We'll do our best, but I think it's gonna be tough, okay? I think we need to be realistic".

Walking over to Joe, I stare down at his face and see that there seems to be a flickering movement under his closed eyelids. "Can he hear us?" I ask.

"No idea," Clyde replies, heading over to the door. "Like I said, I don't have any medical training. I guess it's good that he's stopped bleeding, and I suppose the fact that he seems to be sleeping might be promising. *Might* be, but again, my medical knowledge comes from TV shows. Other than that, your guess is as good as mine. The only thing I know for certain is that we need to get him to a doctor, so let's focus on that, okay? I'm gonna head out and look for a truck. I'll be back soon, okay?"

Once he's gone, I realize I have no idea what to do. Joe's wound still looks deep and bloody, and I figure it should probably be cleaned; at the same time, I have no idea how to do something like that, so I figure I need to leave it alone, in case it starts bleeding again. Reaching out, I feel his forehead and check for a temperature; nothing so far, but I need to keep an eye on him in case he gets some kind of infection. It's not much, but I feel like I have to do something. I've lost both my parents in the past few days, and I can't lose my brother as well.

For the next couple of hours, I try to keep busy. Although I check on Joe regularly, I manage to spend some time out in the street, attempting to learn how to hot-wire a car. While the truck is still broken, Joe reckoned the engine wasn't the problem, so I remove the bodywork under the steering wheel and finally I find the various wires that run to the ignition. I'm not sure I feel confident enough to start ripping them out yet, but eventually I identify two wires that I think might be the ones I need to try. I guess all I need now is to find another vehicle, perhaps a small car, so I can practice.

Sitting up on the driver's seat, I look out the window and spot Clyde heading back this way. I'm about to get out and see if he had any luck, when I narrow my eyes and see that I was wrong: it's not Clyde. It's another, older guy, and he's walking in a kind of slow, jerky manner. Instantly tensing up, I get out of the truck and take a few steps toward him, and that's when I see it: his face has that same green and gray color that I saw on the cop who crawled to our house yesterday. He's walking slowly in my direction, and I take a few steps back, determined to keep a safe distance.

"What do you want?" I ask, glancing over my shoulder to make sure that there's no-one else nearby.

"Ride out of here," he says, his voice

sounding rough. "I need a ride out of here".

"You're sick," I say.

"Who's sick?"

"You're *sick*," I say again. "I can see it".

"I'm not sick. I'm tired, but I'm not sick". He smiles. "I've seen you before, haven't I?"

I shake my head, moving carefully around the truck in order to make sure I keep out of his reach.

"Yeah," the guy continues, "you were in... Tokyo, right? No, that can't be right. London. Bristol. Paris... It's so confusing. Where are we now?" He pauses for a moment, wobbling slightly as he holds the side of the truck. "Oh, yeah, that's right. You set me on fire".
"I don't know what the hell you're talking about," I say, preparing to run inside.

"Yeah, you do," he says. "I was on the ground, and you poured petrol on me and light a match. Let me tell you something, kid, that was quite an experience. I was still getting used to it all. I'm still not quite there yet, but..." He holds up one of his hands and wriggles his fingers. "Even the small things are hard to re-learn, but I'm getting there slowly. I've even learned how to coordinate the others and run them on a kind of auto-pilot. That's impressive, isn't it?"

"I..." I stare at him, and then I turn and run into the house, pushing the door shut as I go and securing the lock. My heart's pounding and I can hear the guy shuffling around outside. After a moment, I hear a knock on the window.

"You don't wanna come out with me?" the guy shouts. "I think we need to talk!"

I draw the curtains, so that at least the guy can't see me. Heading over to Joe, I look down and see that he's still unconscious. There's no way I can move him, not right now, but at the same time I don't see how we can stay here. The guy could easily break the window, and the only thing I can use to defend myself with right now is one of the knives over by the sink.

"Come on!" the guy shouts, pounding on the glass. "Don't make me force my way in there, kid! Be reasonable. After all, *you* set fire to *me*, remember? I'm the one who should be kinda nervous in this situation. Why don't you come out here and hear what I've got to say?"

I stand completely still and listen to the sound of the guy still banging on the window.

"You like setting fire to people, don't you?" he calls out. "I was in the house when you torched the place. Whose body was that, anyway? It's hard to tell, especially when you don't have time to get to a mirror. I got to the door just as you and your brother drove off into the sunset. Is that what you're gonna do this time? You gonna burn me again? I'll just keep coming, so you might as well open the door and talk to me alike an adult".

Hurrying over to the back door, I pull it open and see that there's a small yard to the rear of the building. Just as I'm considering carrying Joe out this way, however, I spot movement over by the gate; seconds later, two more figures appear, one male and one female, and they've both got the same deathly pallor about their faces.

"I've got reinforcements!" the guy calls from the front of the house. "I can see through their eyes!"

"I can move through their bodies," the second guy suddenly says.

"I can talk through their mouths," the woman adds. "Does that freak you out?"

Slamming the door shut, I make sure it's locked before going back over to check on Joe. He seems to be the same as before; my hands are shaking as I realize there's no way I can move him.

"It doesn't matter what you do," the first guy calls out through the window. "You can run, you can hide, you can do absolutely anything. Whatever. I've got strength in numbers, and I'm coming for you. I always knew I wouldn't be able to execute a perfect kill rate, so I anticipated a little mopping up in the aftermath. Just a few thousand odd souls to extinguish before I reach the point of total biological saturation. Don't worry, though. I can make it nice and quick. In one way, you're one of the lucky ones. Then again, in other ways, you're not".

The back door starts to rattle, as the two figures in the yard start trying to get inside.

"There were nearly seven billion people on the planet when this started," the first guy says. "I reckon maybe a few hundred survived. Out of the rest, about half were wasted in the first couple of days while I was still working out how to do all this. Still, that leaves me with, what, about three and a half billion bodies at my disposal? You think you can set us all on fire, kid? Why don't you just accept the inevitable?" He starts banging harder on the window. "Come on, let us in. Don't make us do this the hard way!"

Hurrying to the other side of the kitchen, I start gathering together the biggest knives.

"You're stubborn," the first guy continues. "Let's try a different approach. What's your name?" He waits for me to answer. "Okay, my name's Joseph. We're all Joseph now. It's a long story, but I've been working up to this point for years. The main thing you need to know is, anyone who's not Joseph, is no longer welcome. So why not open up and let's get this done, huh?" There's another pause, and suddenly the window smashes. I see the guy's arm start to reach inside, so I run over and plunge one of the knives into his shoulder.

"No pain," he continues. "That's good. I was

wondering how that'd work, although..." He pulls the arm back outside. "You've damaged a tendon or two. On a purely mechanical level, you've done a bit of a number on me, that's for sure. Still, there's plenty more where that came from". He reaches the other arm inside. "Is this what you want, kid? You want to spend your final moments fighting? Why not just accept your fate? I promise I'll make it painless. If you keep fighting, though, I might let things get a little ugly. After all, you set fire to me, so why shouldn't I do the same to you?"

I step back as he starts trying to climb through the window. Taking a deep breath, I rush forward and push one of the knives straight through the top of his head. He wobbles for a moment, and I take the opportunity to push him back outside.

"Nasty," says the other guy, who's still at the back door. "That felt weird. I've never had a knife stuck in my brain before. I could feel the cold steel digging right down until it hit the base and scraped against the inside of the skull, and then the body died. Wow. I swear, that's one of the freakiest deaths I've had yet. Even worse than the fire incident". He starts shaking the door again. "So come on, kid. You can't keep this up forever. Put down the knives, open the door, and face facts. There's too many of me. I can die billions of times, but you only need to die once. At this very moment, I'm bringing reinforcements from the rest of the town. You can't get away, so open the door and let's find a nice, painless way for you to shuffle off".

I stand in silence, my heart pounding, as I wait for him to make his next move. I don't really understand what the hell he's going on about, but it seems like the same mind is inhabiting all these different bodies.

"Okay," he says eventually. "I see how this is gonna be. You're gonna be a little harder to kill than some of the others. Fine. Let's do it your way, but I hope you've got a lot of knives ready, 'cause we're coming in and we're not gonna be -" Suddenly he stops talking, and I hear two loud thuds.

Hearing a sound over at the window, I turn and get ready to attack again, but at the last moment I see that this time it's Clyde who's clambering through.

"Where the hell have you been?" I shout.

"There's things out there!" he replies, struggling to his feet. There's a knife in his hand. "They're headed this way. I just took two of 'em down at the back door, but there's a load more all over town".

"We need to get out of here," I tell him. "Help me move Joe!"

"And go where?" Clyde shouts, clearly starting to panic. "The truck doesn't work, so where the hell are we gonna go?" He pauses for a moment. "The only thing we can do is run. We have to get as many supplies as possible and we have to run, and we have to hope these things can't chase after us".

"Joe can't run," I point out.

"Then Joe ain't coming," Clyde replies, hurrying over to the window just as two more of the creatures appear. Stepping back, he turns to me. "I came back to get you because I thought you might be useful," he says, as the creatures start trying to climb through the window. "But I'm not risking my life just to carry your fucking brother anywhere". Grabbing one of the knives from the table, he heads over to the window and pushes the blade into the first creature's head, before pulling it out and doing the same to the second. Once he's pushed them both back, he turns to me. "There's no time to waste, kid. You coming, or not?"

"I can't leave Joe," I reply.

"Fine," he says, turning and starting to climb out the window. "You'll -" He stops suddenly, and then he moves back inside as another creature appears outside. "There's loads of 'em!" he shouts. "They're everywhere!"

Hearing a banging sound from the back door, I run to the other window and look out to see a handful of the creatures making their way toward the building, walking obliviously past the corpses of the two that Clyde killed a moment ago.

"Now what?" Clyde shouts.

DAY 8

ELIZABETH

Manhattan

"I KNOW YOU'RE AWAKE," Bob says calmly. "I can tell from the way you're breathing. When you were unconscious, you were breathing kinda slow and steady, but about a minute ago it changed and became faster. So that's how I know. I've studied this kind of thing. You're not fooling anyone, so you might as well just stop the charade and look at me". Silence for a moment. "Look at me, Elizabeth".

Slowly, I raise my head, open my heavy eyes, and stare straight at Bob.

"That's better," he says with a smile. "That's a lot better".

We're in a room at the back of the building, and I'm tied to the same chair where Bob previously held Mallory. Thick ropes are wrapped tightly around my body, and there's a gag over my mouth. My heart is racing so fast, it's like a continual, pounding patter in my chest, and I feel like I'm about to pass out at any moment.

"One week," Bob says, turning and walking across the darkened room. The only light comes from a series of small windows at the top of the far wall. "Did you know that? It's been exactly one week since all of this started to happen. Well, almost. Today is day eight. One week ago, was day one". He checks his watch. "It's about two hours until the *exact* one week anniversary, which I propose to mark with a glass of scotch. Do you remember what you were doing this time a week ago, Elizabeth? I guess you were probably getting on with your dull, mundane little life. Doing all those things that turned out not to be too important in the grand scheme of things. Hanging out with friends who're probably dead now".

Staring at him, I realize he's gloating. He actually seems to be happy with how things are right now.

"Do you know what I was doing a week ago?" he asks. "I was just getting on with things. Being ignored, although that didn't matter to me too much. I didn't mind. I was busy, you see. I was preparing for a change in the world. I saw it coming. I looked at the world and I saw that we were headed for disaster. Sure, I didn't know what form that disaster was gonna take, but I could see it coming, clear as day. A virus, or a computer fuck-up, or something nuclear. I knew we were gonna screw ourselves, and finally it happened. But while most of you people were stunned and unprepared, I was ready. I'd stock-piled. I'd thought ahead. So you see, suddenly it became very clear that I'm not a loser after all. I win. I sacrificed certain things in the old world in order to be ready for the new". He smiles. "Betcha feeling just a little pissed off right now, aren't you?"

I take a deep breath, trying to work out how I'm going to get free. All I can think is that I need Henry to come and find me, but I have no idea where my brother is right now, and I doubt Bob's gonna allow him to just set me free.

"Huh," Bob continues, tapping at the face of his watch. "Do you ever think about things like this? I mean, a watch is a simple thing, but eventually the battery's gonna stop, and then it won't work. It'll just be a chunk of dead cogs and stuff. All across America, maybe even the world, clocks are eventually going to stop. We're literally running out of time". He pauses. "You know what'd be good? One of those watches you wind up. They don't need batteries. That's something I should have got, before the world turned to shit. Well, I guess everyone has to overlook something. No-one's perfect".

Moving my arms a little, I find that the ropes are tied far too tight for me to be able to wriggle free. Even if Bob left me alone for an entire day, I don't think I could get away.

"I'm rambling," he says after a moment. "I doubt you care much about my ruminations on time, that sort of thing. We should probably just get straight down to business". He walks over to a nearby bench, from which he takes a hammer. "Your decision to free that Mallory girl has been weighing on my mind," he says eventually, carrying the hammer back over to me. "It's been bothering me. It was a supremely disloyal act, Elizabeth. It was a sign that you don't understand whose side you're on, and that you can't be trusted". Leaning down, he places the head of the hammer against my left kneecap and gives it a gentle tap. "If I kneecapped you," he continues, "you wouldn't be able to betray me again, would you?" He continues to tap my kneecap with the hammer, using a little more force each time. As he starts to smile, the tapping reaches the point where it starts to hurt; just as I'm getting worried, he abruptly stops and carries the hammer back over to the bench.

"Did you think I was gonna do it?" he calls back to me, as he sorts through some of the other tools. "Did you think I was gonna smash your kneecaps into tiny pieces?" He pauses. "I considers it. I'm still considering it. The truth is, I can see a benefit to killing you, but also a benefit to keeping you alive for a little torture. You see, I'd never tortured anyone before Mallory showed up, and that didn't last long, so you're really my first chance. I don't *want* to torture anyone, but I feel I should get to know how it's done, in case I have to do it later. I should make sure I know which parts of the body to attack first, to cause maximum pain". He picks up a hacksaw.

Still struggling to get my arms free, I watch as Bob continues to examine his tools. I'm starting to get more and more worried: this guy is just crazy enough to step over the line. I saw what he did to Mallory, and with me he's got the added incentive of some kind of personal vendetta.

"The thought of hurting someone is... horrifying," he continues. "The thought of cutting someone's foot off, for example, while they're screaming for mercy. That's just awful. But I feel as if this empathy is a weakness. Maybe if I do something like that, I'll be able to streamline my reactions. Numb myself, you know? Become a good soldier, because God knows, right now I'm not a good soldier. I try my best, but I still have these weaknesses". He brings the hacksaw over and holds the rusty blade against my ankle. "What if I'm in a combat situation, and I pause before delivering the fatal blow? Just a fraction of a second could make all the difference. I need to make sure I don't flinch". He presses the blade harder against my skin. "I don't want to do it to you, of course, but maybe that's exactly why I *should*. Maybe my reluctance is the problem. If I were to torture you, really go at you, I might improve my ability to function as a warrior".

I take a deep breath, trying to calm down. There's got to be a way out of this; I just have to work out what to do next.

"Touch choices," Bob says, heading back over to the bench. "I'm gonna have to think long and hard about this, aren't I? I'm gonna have to decide what kind of person I want to be. I think I can change, if that's what's necessary. I can become the kind of man I want to be. After all those years of sitting around, being ignored, I can finally carve out a place for myself in the world".

I look over at the door. I figure Henry has to come back here at some point. I just need to wait it out until he finds me. I mean, sure, Henry's allowed himself to be seduced by Bob's offers of power, but he hasn't become a monster. When he sees his own sister tied up like this, about to be hurt, he's gonna act. He won't let Bob do this to me.

"I like the world like this," Bob says eventually. "I'm sorry, but I do. I like the fact that most of everyone has dropped dead. I like the fact that suddenly we've got a little space and time. I like the fact that a man can make his own decisions and his own choices, rather than relying on other people". He picks up a gun from the bench. "I like the fact that we're all in charge of our own destiny". He puts down the gun and picks up a large hunting knife. "I like the fact that the weak are gonna die off and the strong are gonna show their worth. That's how it should be. The problem with the old world was that we'd stopped punishing the weak and the stupid. You could be a fucking idiot, but you'd still be carried along by society. We needed something like this, to prune out the morons. Now there'll just be the cream of the crop left, and we can start to improve the stock".

He puts the knife down, and then he comes back over to me. Kneeling in front of me, he places his hands on my knees.

"Despite our differences, Elizabeth, I can see that you're a smart girl. That's why I think you can be rehabilitated. You can be brought back into the fold, and then we can see about using your smarts for good". He gently moves my knees apart. "We have a duty to restock the human race, Elizabeth. I've been reading up on childbirth. That library of Mr. Blake's was pretty useful in the end. Ultimately, I think what we're gonna have to do is we're gonna have to make sure you pop out some babies, so we can start a new generation. Obviously you can't have your own brother be the father, so I think that leaves only one option. I'm sure you'll get used to it eventually. It's not so bad. I know I'm not your type. You probably like cool young dudes with spiky hair and pierced what-nots. But that was when sex was for pleasure. Now it's a duty to the whole human race, or what's left of it".

Standing up, he pats his large belly.

"I'm hungry," he says, before walking around me, grabbing the back of the chair, and turning me around until I'm facing the other side of the room. A few meters away, there's a series of tables covered in sheets.

"You hungry?" he asks, walking over to another bench and grabbing a carving knife. He checks the sharpness of the blade. "Time for steak," he adds, before heading to the first table and reaching out, ready to pull the sheet away. "The human must change," he says after a moment, staring down at the table. "Things that seemed abominable and wrong before, must now be accepted. Again, it's a matter of perseverance; you do something enough times, it stops being bad. You start to tolerate it, and then eventually you might even get to the point where you enjoy it. You know what I'm saying. And frankly, I'd rather eat good, healthy meat than pre-packaged shit any day. At least there's no tiny surveillance devices in fresh meat, right?" Smiling, he pulls the sheet away to reveal a large, pink, bloody chunk of meat.

It takes me a moment to realize what I'm staring at. My first assumption is that it's a pig, that Bob has somehow managed to get hold of an actual pig, or maybe a cow carcass, and he's been cutting it up for food. After a moment, however, the kinda abstract shape starts to become more recognizable: I see large, dark red slices where the arms and legs have been removed, leaving just a torso, and the head is also missing. There are a couple of nipples on top, though, and at the other end there's a penis. I keep trying to tell myself that I'm wrong, that this isn't what I think it is, but my eyes widen as I realize that it's a human body.

"You remember Mr. Blake, don't you?" Bob says, staring down at the corpse. "I couldn't let him leave us. I couldn't let all that meat and nutrition go walking out the door. I've got pretty good at not wasting anything. Even the bones, I boil 'em down to make broth. I swear, not a part of this man has gone to waste, except a few bits like the guts, 'cause obviously there's basic hygiene to consider".

Unable to contain my panic, I start struggling to get free from the chair.

"Relax," Bob says with a grin, "you haven't personally eaten any of Mr. Blake. Not yet, anyway. Henry and I have had that pleasure". He walks over to the next table, pulls the sheet away, and reveals another torso, except this one is almost picked clean, with the rib cage showing. "This is the one you ate from when you had steak a few days ago. You remember Mrs. DeWitt from upstairs, right? She was old, of course, but her meat was surprisingly tender once I'd marinaded it properly". He pulls the final sheets away, to reveal another torso, this time with most of the meat left on its bones. "And that's old Albert Carling. I didn't want to waste him, either". He reaches down, pulls a piece of meat from Albert's bones, and pops it into his mouth.

As I try to get away from the chair, I accidentally tip myself over, landing hard against the concrete floor. Despite the gag over my mouth, I try to call out for help as Bob walks slowly over to me.

"A human body gives up some good meat," he says. "And you know what? It's not bad for us. Not at all. You ate meat from Mrs. DeWitt's body, Elizabeth, several times. If I'd told you it was human flesh, you'd have turned it down, but you accepted it, you even enjoyed it, because I told you it was normal cow meat. So, you see, most of this is about perception. You perceived it to be beef, and your brain let you enjoy it". He reaches down and pulls my chair back up until I'm sitting again. "This is the food chain now," he continues. "You turn it down, you starve. Don't let your old world fears and prejudices affect how you act in the new world, Elizabeth. Face the reality of the situation. It's really not so bad".

After checking his watch, he grabs the back of my chair and turns me back to face the other way.

"There," he says. "Maybe we'll save dinner until a bit later, huh? Now, I've got to go and check the perimeter, but you're gonna sit here and think about what I've said. Be smart, Elizabeth. This doesn't have to be painful or hard. Just accept that things have changed. Think about it. This time in a year, you could be the proud mother of the next generation of the human race, and..." He laughs. "Well, that's gonna happen, really, whether you like it or not. I'm not gonna jeopardize the future of humanity just 'cause you're a little weak-willed. But it'd be easier if you're onside for this stuff, yeah? Much easier, and much more pleasant. Hell, you might even start to enjoy yourself eventually. What's the alternative? Live the rest of your life in misery?"

I watch as he heads over to the door.

"I'll be back in a few hours," he says, turning to glance back at me. "We'll get started".

Once he's gone, I sit and stare straight ahead. This room is so dark and so isolated, I feel like there's no way I'm ever going to escape. Behind me, those three dead bodies are still on display, waiting for Bob to carve more meat from the bones. After desperately struggling to get loose from the ropes for a few minutes, I start to realize that there's no way out. With the gag still over my mouth, I start calling out for help, hoping that someone - anyone - might eventually hear me.

THOMAS

Oklahoma

"THEY STILL OUT THERE?" I ask, watching as Clyde stands by the window.

"What do you think?" he replies, turning to me. There's a haunted look on his face, as if he knows that we're screwed.

"What are they doing?"

"Same as they've been doing all night. Just, like, milling about". He pauses. "It's weird. It's like they're just mindlessly loitering. It's like they're waiting for something".

"They're waiting for *him*," I say, feeling a sense of panic rise through my body. I still haven't worked out exactly what's happening, but one thing's for certain: it's as if all these creatures have the same mind, as if that mind can experience things through all the creatures simultaneously. How that works, and how it happened, I don't know, but I've seen it with my own eyes: what one of the creatures experiences, they all experience, and they share one another's memories. Talking to one of them is like talking to all of them, which makes it especially weird that they seem, all at once, to have suddenly gone silent.

"Waiting for who?" Clyde asks.

"The guy who's behind it," I say, immediately regretting my choice of words. Damn it, I probably sound like some kind of paranoid idiot. "I mean, the person who..." My voice trails off as I try to think of a way to explain it properly. I haven't even managed to get it straight in my own head yet, so telling someone else about my theory is pretty difficult. "You haven't talked to any of them?" I ask eventually.

"I didn't know it was possible," he replies.

"It is. They can talk, and when they do, it's like they all have the same mind. There was one here, last night, who remembered talking to me back at our farm, when I talked to one of the others. It's like they have this shared memory".

Clyde stares at me, as if I've just come out with the craziest stuff he's ever heard. I guess that's probably true enough.

"I know it sounds insane," I continue, "but

I've seen it with my own eyes. They've got this kind of group mentality thing going on. They can carry on the same conversation from one body to the next".

"I don't get it," Clyde says.

"Neither do I. It doesn't make sense, but if you talk to them, that's what happens".

"So why are they just standing out there now?" he asks. "If they're so fucking organized, why are they just hanging around as if they've got nothing to do? It looks like someone flicked the off-switch on 'em all".

Hurrying around the kitchen table, I lean across the counter and peer into the street. It's still only just getting light out there, but I can see scores of the creatures, all standing around as if they're waiting for someone to tell them what to do. They're just standing in the street, like drones awaiting orders. They've been like this all night, but I'm convinced they'll spring back to life as soon as we head outside. Unfortunately, with Joe still unconscious and flat on his back on the table, there's no way we can move fast enough to escape them. Joe's injuries are too bad, and the last thing he needs right now is to be picked up and carried anywhere.

"They're so fucking creepy," Clyde says. "I recognize some of them. They're like rotted versions of people I used to see around town. That one over there, in the blue shirt? That's Frank Ottowitz, the guy who used to run the diner. The one next to him, that's Ginny Ladler, from the school. It's like dead bodies are wandering the streets. Do you think it's..." He pauses for a moment. "I mean, don't laugh, but do you think it..."

"What?"

"Well, do you think it's zombies?"

"Zombies?" I ask, turning to him.

"Well, I mean, they look like zombies," he continues. "They're all rotted and stuff, like zombies. Isn't that what zombies are?"

"Zombies aren't real," I point out.

"Well, those things are," he says, "and I reckon they fit the bill for zombies". He pauses for a moment. "That one you talked to, did he say anything about wanting to eat our brains?"

"No," I say firmly. "Of course he didn't". "Then what did he want with you?"

"He wanted to kill us," I say. "He kept going on about finishing some job he'd started. I didn't really understand the whole thing, but it was as if he saw us as an annoyance".

He sniffs. "Looks like a zombie. Acts like a zombie. Sounds like a zombie. Maybe they actually -"

"They're not zombies!" I tell him. "They're just... things. They're something, but they're not zombies".

"Whatever," he replies, "we need to get out of here. We've waited long enough. I don't know why they've all just stopped out there like that, but it's not gonna be permanent. Besides, we need food and water. This situation's unsustainable. If we're quick and we plan it, I think we can make it to the truck".

"We can't move Joe," I say, looking down at my brother. Although his wound has stopped bleeding, he's still badly hurt and I'm worried that any attempt to get him out onto the truck would make things worse. "Anyway," I add, "the truck's damaged. Unless you know how to fix it, we're stuck here".

"Then we'll die," Clyde says. "Simple as that. We'll starve and we'll die, or they'll decide to come after us again. Is that what you want? You want to stay around here and wait for those things to decide they want to come in and get us after all?"

"I can't leave my brother," I reply.

"*I* can leave him".

"Then you can go".

"I'm just saying, he's pretty much..." He looks down at Joe. "Don't get me wrong, Thomas. Your brother seemed like an okay kind of guy. A bit blunt at times, but that's not so bad. Still, we've gotta face facts. He's hurt, and he's hurt bad. Look at him. You know he's not gonna get better. You can stand around being a good brother all you like, but it's not gonna change anything. With those injuries, he'll be lucky to last another day".

"If you want to run, then run, but I have to stay here until he gets better".

"You're insane. Look at him. He's not gonna get better, not now, not ever. Even if we could get him to a state-of-the-art hospital, he'd struggle to pull through. I think you're gonna have to face facts, kid. Your brother's not gonna get out of this, and we -"

"He just needs time," I say, although I know it's not true. Clyde's right: if we just sit around here like this, Joe's going to die. The gashed wound in his side isn't the kind of thing that'll just heal by itself. We need to come up with a better plan, but it's looking increasingly as if there's no way out. I keep thinking that if I just wait long enough, I'll come up with a new idea, but deep down I know that's not gonna happen. I guess I'm just delaying the inevitable moment when I have to leave him behind.

"I'm gonna look for some more towels," Clyde says. "You're gonna need 'em to deal with the bleeding if it starts up again. But after that, I'm out of here. I already made one mistake by agreeing to stay an extra night with you guys. I'm not gonna do the same thing again, okay? If you don't come with me today, you're on your own".

"How are you gonna get away?"

He shrugs. "I'll outrun the fuckers if I have to. Whatever. I'd rather die fighting than just sit around here, waiting to be picked off".

Once he's gone upstairs, I take another quick look out the window and see that the creatures are still just loitering as if they're awaiting orders. There's something not quite right about this whole situation; I don't get why they aren't trying to get inside, and I don't get why the voice doesn't seem to want to talk anymore. Yesterday, it seemed as if they were determined to get in here, and then they just stopped. There's enough of them out there that they could just rush the building and break in, if they all attacked together, but they're clearly waiting for something.

Sighing, I walk over to the kitchen table and check on Joe. The wound in his side is caked thick with congealed, dark red blood, and splintered pieces of bone are protruding at several spots. Reaching down, I check his forehead and feel a slight temperature. If he's getting an infection, there's nothing else we can do for him apart from trying to make him comfortable. He hasn't woken up since the accident, and I feel like he's sinking deeper and deeper into a sleep from which he'll never wake up. His pulse seems weak, and his breathing's shallow. He's slowly dying, and right now I can't think of a single way to help him.

Deciding that I need to see if Clyde has

anything I can use for antiseptic, I head through to the back-room, hoping that maybe Clyde has a liquor cabinet. There's nothing there, of course; the most I can find is an old, half-finished carton of orange juice, but I doubt that's gonna be much use for Joe. In fact, Clyde's whole house seems to be strangely bare, as if the guy just lived alone and didn't have much need for things like furniture. He's got the bare essentials, but the place doesn't really feel as if anyone lived here. I can't shake the feeling that the whole house was a mess long before all of this stuff started to happen.

As I continue to explore, I find a small door that leads into a large lock-up garage. To my surprise, I see that there's a truck parked in here, which seems more than a little strange, seeing as Clyde's been going on and on about how a working truck is *exactly* the kind of thing we need to find. I wander over to the truck and look through the window; there are some maps strewn on one of the seats, and an old paper coffee cup is sitting on the dashboard. There doesn't seem to be any obvious reason why this thing isn't up and running, though I suppose there could be some damage under the hood. If this thing works, it's our ticket out of here, but I guess there must be a problem with it. After all, there's no way Clyde would have failed to mention a working truck. Not unless he's hoarding it for himself, after all. Then again, if that was the case, why did he try to steal *our* truck the other day?

Pausing for a moment, I realize that nothing about Clyde really makes sense. I still don't quite understand why he tried to take our truck, and I still don't quite get why he's still here. After all, he keeps going on about how he's got no loyalty to Joe and about how he's ready to make a run for it, yet he's still here; still bitching and complaining, but still here. It's like he's just hanging around for no particular reason; at the best of times, none of this would make much sense, but the urgency of the situation makes Clyde's behavior seem particularly weird. He's not acting like someone who's genuinely terrified of what's happening; in fact, he seems as if he's determined to hang around, despite having plenty of opportunities to get away. Something's not right about him, and I feel like it's time to find out if I can really trust him.

ELIZABETH

Manhattan

IT'S TAKEN A COUPLE of hours, but I feel as if I've finally managed to get one of my hands loose. Partially loose, anyway. I've pushed and pushed and pushed against the rope, and finally I've created a little extra room, in which I can turn my wrist. It's not much, but it's a start. In the process, I've managed to give myself a slight rope-burn around the side of my hands, but I don't care about that right now; I just need to get free.

"You're doing okay," a voice says suddenly. "Another couple of days and you might actually get somewhere".

I stop moving. Footsteps approach me from behind, and finally Henry walks in front of me.

"Sorry," he says. "I've been watching you for a while. I just wanted to see what you might be able to do".

"Get me out of here!" I try to say, although the gag turns this into little more than a blurred collection of murmurs.

"Bob was right," he continues. "You need to face reality. You're living in the new world, but with the same mind you used in the old world. You need to transition from one mindset to the next, and it'll take a while for you to complete that... to complete that process of change and... transformation".

I stare at him, as he struggles to remember every word of the spiel he's learned from Bob. It's like he's been brain-washed, to the extent that he seems to totally accept everything Bob does and says. He doesn't seem to be bothered by the dead bodies on the tables behind me, or by Bob's collection of saws and other torture devices. I'm starting to seriously wonder whether my little brother's head is in the right place, and whether there's any hope that I might be able to bring him back to a more rational place.

"Where'd you go?" he asks after a moment, and finally I start to see a little of his real personality shining through. "You were gone, like, more than a day. Where the hell were you?"

I mumble something under the gag.

"I can't..." He pauses, and then he checks over his shoulder before stepping behind me and starting to untie the gag. "If you shout, I'll put it back on," he says quietly. "If you call for help, same. You have to speak quietly, okay? Bob doesn't want me doing this". He slips the gag away.

"Get me out of here," I say, quietly and quickly.

"I can't".

"Henry!"

"I *can't*! It's Bob's decision!"

"Bullshit. Untie me, Henry. Please. The guy's insane. You saw what he did to Mallory. He's gonna do the same to me, or worse. You didn't hear what he told me earlier. He wants to -"

"Yeah, I heard," he replies.

I take a deep breath. "You heard?"

"I was here".

Sighing, I realize Henry was skulking in the shadows the whole time. I'd hoped that I could appeal to him by making him understand the truth about Bob's intentions, but now I realize that Henry already knows the truth. It's not that he doesn't see what's happening; it's that he sees what's happening, and he's accepted it. I don't know quite how Bob has done it, but Henry seems to have been persuaded that black is white and right is wrong.

"Those steaks..." I say. "They're human".

"I know," Henry says. "The food chain has

changed, Elizabeth. You have to -"

"I heard," I reply firmly. "Bob said the exact same thing. The *exact* same thing. You're like a little fucking robot, parroting everything he says. Don't you ever think for yourself these days?"

"Bob's right," he says. "I can't help it if what I think happens to be the same as what he thinks. It's natural that two intelligent people should reach the same conclusion".

I sigh, realizing that I'm getting nowhere with this approach. "What's he offered you, Henry?" I ask after a moment. "A gun? A uniform? Unlimited food?" I pause for a moment. "I met some people. They're heading west to start a new life by Lake Ontario. I could have gone with them, but I chose to stay behind because I wanted to come back and get you. We can still follow them, though. You and me, away from this place. The city's dangerous, Henry. We don't need Bob!"

"We can't just go wandering off across the country," he replies. "That's suicide".

"No," I say, "staying here is suicide". "Then why did you? You had a chance to leave, so why didn't you take it? If this is so bad, why'd you come back?"

"Because of you!"

He stares at me, as if he can't quite believe what I'm saying.

"I came back because of you," I continue. "I

came back because you're my brother, and because I know you're not gonna let Bob do this. You heard him. He wants to sleep with me and get me pregnant so we can start a new generation. The guy's crazy, Henry. There are rats all over the place. There's gonna be disease everywhere soon, and the city's gonna become like a cesspit. If we stay here, we'll die a slow, horrible death. Bob's crazy. He thinks he's the king of this castle, but he's got nothing. What's he gonna do when he finishes eating those bodies? Where's he gonna get his next meat from? Rats?"

"Bob's got everything under control," Henry says, sounding a little defensive. It's as if I've finally started to get through to him.

"Bob's an ass," I say. "He doesn't understand. He thinks he's got the world sorted out, but he's just living on this island that's getting smaller and smaller. He thinks he's justified in hurting people and killing people and eating people, but it's all in his head. If we get out of here, we can go follow the others, Mallory and the others, and we can maybe find somewhere we can really start over. Mom and Dad aren't coming back -"
"They might," he snaps back at me.

"No," I say. "Really not. You're just saying that because it's an excuse to sit here and hope for a miracle. They're gone, Henry, and we have to do what's right for us. We have to get the hell out of this place".

"Bob said you'd say that," he replies. There's definitely a new sense of uncertainty in his eyes, as if he's starting to doubt the things he's saying.

"You know what Bob's gonna do to me?" I ask, deciding it's time to really ram things home. "He's gonna torture me a little, just to soften me up, and then he's gonna have sex with me so he can -"

Henry shakes his head.

"So he can get me pregnant with his little Bob spawn, and he thinks we're gonna build this new civilization, and all the while we're gonna be eating those dead bodies behind me -"

"No," Henry says, his voice faltering. "That's not what's gonna happen".

"It's exactly what he said he's gonna do!" I reply, raising my voice a little. "You heard him! Word for word, that's what he's gonna do! Think about it, Henry. He's gonna get on top of me and have sex with me on the pretext of somehow saving civilization, and we're gonna stay in this building while a rising tide of filth and disease surrounds us, and eventually we'll be stuck here like we're on an island, except the filth and the rats are gonna start coming higher and higher up the building until we'll be up on the roof with nowhere to go!"

"No," Henry says again.

"Yes!"

"Why?" Henry replies. "Why would Bob do

that? Why would Bob do something that's gonna end up like that? He wouldn't. He's got a plan -"

"Because he's unhinged," I say. "Because he thinks he's the leader of some new, brave world that's gonna rise from the ashes of what we used to have. It's not gonna work, Henry. Look at this place. It's been one week since everything started. The people I met, Mallory and the others, are setting off to start a new life outside the city. Bob, meanwhile, has already got you eating human meat, with a gun in your hand, while he plans to hurt your own sister". I pause for a moment, hoping my words might sink in. "Bob's right when he says things have to change," I continue eventually, "but his version of that change is totally, completely wrong".

Henry stares at me, as if he's finally starting to really think about what I'm saying. I hate seeing him like this, lost and confused, but it's the only way I'm ever going to get him away from Bob.

"Untie me," I say firmly, "and we'll get out of here. We won't hurt Bob. We won't even take any of his food or his other supplies. We'll just leave, and we'll go catch up to the others. There's still time, Henry. You're not locked into this".

"I can't leave Bob alone," he says. "I can let you go, but I have to stay".

I shake my head.

"Why not?" he asks.

"Because you're my brother," I tell him.

He sighs.

"I'm sticking with you," I say. "I'm not leaving you with this madman. If I have to, I'll..." I pause, as I realize that I might be forced to take drastic action if I'm gonna get Henry away from Bob. After all, if Bob died, there'd be nothing to keep Henry here. I hate the idea of killing someone, but if that's the price I have to pay in order to get Henry out of here, then I guess it's something I'll have to do. "Untie me," I say. "We'll stay, at least for a couple of days".

He stares at me.

"Henry, we -"

"I'll let you go," he says, suddenly, hurrying behind me and starting to loosen the ropes.

"What about you?" I ask, pulling my hands free as Henry starts working on the ropes around my legs.

"I'm gonna persuade Bob to come with us," he says.

"Henry -"

"He'll come around," he continues. "He'll see that we have to leave the city. He's not an idiot. I'll explain it to him. He'll get it, he has to".

"And if he doesn't?" I ask, standing up.

"He will".

Hurrying over to the bench, I reach out to grab the gun before pausing for a moment. There's something about guns that I really, really hate. I grab a knife instead, figuring that at least a knife has uses other than just to kill.

"This way," Henry says, grabbing my hand and dragging me across the room.

"Where are we going?" I ask.

"You're gonna get out of here and wait for us," he says. "I'm gonna find Bob and make him understand what we have to do".

We head through to the yard, and then into the back of the restaurant. Hurrying across the empty kitchen, we eventually reach a small side door that should lead into the main dining area and then, eventually, to the street.

"Can you wait here?" Henry asks. "I won't need long".

"You can't trust Bob," I say.

"I can".

"You can't. If you try to reason with him -"

"Trust *me*!" he shouts. "Trust me that I can make him see sense. Bob's not my boss. I wasn't working with him 'cause he brainwashed me, I was working with him because I agreed with him. We're equals. I can make him see sense. We'll leave all of this behind, but we're taking Bob with us".

"Is that right?" calls out a voice from nearby.

Turning, I see that Bob is standing a few meters away, a grin on his face and his rifle pointed straight at us.

"I was just coming to find you," Henry

stutters, with panic in his eyes.

"So I heard," Bob replies. "I heard the whole damn caboodle. I've gotta say, Henry, I'm a little disappointed in the way your sister here was able to turn you so easily. I thought you'd put up more of a fight, but I figured I'd better test you first. That's why I left you alone with her. I'm sorry to say, you failed that test miserably".

"It's not like that," Henry says, stepping toward him. "I just listened to what she said, and maybe she's right".

"You're allowing old world feelings to cloud your judgment," Bob says. "You're not seeing the world as it truly is, Henry. Just because she's your sister, doesn't mean you have to swallow her bullshit. Do you really think the best option is just to go running out of the city and into the wilderness like fucking apes? Abandon everything we've got here? All that stuff about disease, that's not gonna happen. It *could*, but it won't. You know *why* it won't? 'Cause I've got a fucking plan. I'm gonna deal with it. I'm gonna stop it. I'm gonna make sure we're all safe. I just need some people with me who actually believe in what I'm doing, rather than having their head turned by their sister."

"But if we leave -" Henry starts to say.

"You know what?" Bob replies, interrupting him. "This whole family thing is overblown anyway. Brother, sister, all that shit. It's a relic of an old world. Who gives a shit whether you came out of the same birth canal? You're individuals. You're not joined at the hip. Elizabeth shouldn't mean any more or any less to you than me, or than Mallory, or than anyone. No-one bound to make dumb-ass decisions just 'cause they've got these stupid family ties".

"Henry," I say, "let's just go. If Bob wants to sit around here and rot, let him. But we need to -"

"Shoot her," Bob says suddenly.

Henry turns to him.

"What?" I say, my heart turning to ice.

"You hear me, boy," Bob continues, staring at Henry. "You've got a weapon. You know how to use it. I'm giving you a direct order. Elizabeth is a threat to our survival. She's shown time and again that she's not a team player. She hid the existence of that little library up in Harrison Blake's room and, more seriously, she went directly against my orders and freed that Mallory girl. Now she's trying to foment revolution. It's time to get rid of her, and throwing her out the door clearly ain't gonna work. So I'm telling you. Shoot her".

Henry turns to look at me, and I can see that he's torn.

"You can't seriously be considering doing this," I say, starting to back away.

Slowly, Henry aims the rifle at me.

"Henry -"

"Every second you wait," Bob says, interrupting, "is another question about your loyalty".

"Henry," I shout, "don't listen to him!"

"Family don't mean a thing," Bob continues. "If she wasn't your sister, you'd have no hesitation in gunning her down, so put all that familial bullshit to one side. In the world today, your family are the people who stand beside you, not the people who happen to have been born to the same bloodline". He pauses, waiting for Henry to pull the trigger. "If family's so fucking important," Bob says after a moment, "then how come it's basically a fucking accident of fate, huh? Why the hell are you supposed to be loyal and devoted to someone based on a fucking fluke?"

Henry stares at me, with the rifle pointed straight at my head.

"Henry -" I say.

"I'm sorry," he whispers, before turning, aiming the rifle straight at Bob, and pulling the trigger.

Nothing.

Just a clicking sound.

Bob stares at Henry for a moment, and finally a smile starts to spread on his face. "Just as I thought," he says eventually. "No fucking loyalty. You can't imagine how bad I felt, boy, when I emptied your gun this morning. But now I see I was right to do it".

"Henry, let's go," I say, reaching out and grabbing my brother's arm.

"Fuck you," Bob says, pulling a handgun from his pocket, aiming it at us and firing.

"Get out of the way!" I shout, pulling Henry away, but I'm not quick enough. The bullet hits him square in the chest and he jolts backward, landing with a heavy thud against the concrete floor.

THOMAS

Oklahoma

"THAT OLD THING?" Clyde smiles, but it's an awkward smile, as if he's been caught out. "Yeah, that doesn't work. It's had problems for years".

"But it *might* work," I say, eying him suspiciously. "I mean, it's worth a shot. What's wrong with it?"

"It won't start".

"So there's a problem with the ignition?"

"Maybe".

"Or the motor?"

He shrugs.

"And you never got it checked out?"

"Not really," he says. "I guess I always thought I had a little time to do it, but then things kind of snowballed". He pauses for a moment. "So, anyway, I found a bunch of towels. You're gonna need them if your brother starts bleeding. Not that they'll do much good, but it's better than nothing, right? I mean, blood's better in than out".

Heading over to the little key-hanger by the door, I quickly find what appears to be a key to Clyde's truck. Removing it from the hanger, I hold it up for him to see. "This the right one?"

He nods, but he doesn't seem sure.

"You mind if I go and give it a try?"

"It doesn't work," he says.

"What doesn't?" I ask, feeling that he's being deliberately vague. "The truck or the key?"

"The truck. The truck doesn't work".

"Huh". I put the key in my pocket. "So are you going now?"

"Me?"

"You said you were gonna get towels, and then you were gonna get out of here".

He sighs. "I guess that was bravado. I mean, how the hell am I gonna get past those things out there?"

"They're just standing around," I point out.

"And you think they'll *keep* just standing around if one of us goes out there?"

"Then you can out-run them," I say. "You managed it before".

"Yeah, but they're... There's so many of

them, Thomas. There must be forty, fifty of the damn things. I'm not exactly in the prime of life. I can run down the street, but if they keep up, I'm gonna be screwed".

"Then what's your plan?" I ask. Something's definitely, definitely not right here. Clyde's inconsistent. He says one thing, then he says another. He says he wants to get out of here, but then he comes up with reasons why he has to stay. I know it's dangerous to assume that everyone's gonna be logical all the time, but I still feel as if there are hidden undercurrents with Clyde, as if there's some unspoken problem that's affecting his decisions. I don't trust the guy at all, and I'm pretty sure he's hiding something.

"I don't really *have* a plan," he says eventually. "My plan was for our brother to fix the truck, and then we'd get out of here". "Which truck?" I ask. "Our truck, or your truck?"

"I don't *have* a truck," he says, seeming a little annoyed. "That's why I tried to take *your* truck the other day".

"But you *do* have a truck". "It doesn't work!" He pauses. "Okay, I should have maybe asked your brother to take a look at mine, but I figured he was gonna get yours working eventually, and I didn't know those things were gonna turn up outside". He looks down at Joe. "I don't know if this is the right time to say this," he adds, "but your brother's getting sick. Real sick. Sicker than ever. I think we need to start preparing for the worst".

"He's not gonna die," I say, momentarily angry before I realize that Clyde seems to be trying to distract me. My questions have definitely rattled him, and I'm starting to see that I need to come up with a plan. "Do you have any spare bed-sheets?" I ask after a moment.

"Bed-sheets?"

I nod, reaching into my pocket and feeling the key to Clyde's truck. I need to hope and pray that this is the right key, and that the truck works properly. Right now, that thing is our only ticket out of Scottsville, and I don't have time to come up with a back-up plan.

"What do you want bed-sheets for?" "I want to make Joe more comfortable. I was thinking of moving the table into your front-room, if that's okay? It's kinda cold through here".

"You think?"

I nod.

Clyde stares at me for a moment. "I guess," he says cautiously. "I can go look for bed-sheets. They're probably upstairs, I'll..." He pauses again, as if he's trying to work out what I'm planning. "I'll go get them".

"I'm gonna move the table," I say.

"You want help?"

"No," I say quickly. "I can do it".

"I'll just be a couple of minutes," he says, before heading over to the foot of the stairs. He glances back at me, as if he's started to realize that I'm up to something. For a moment, I think he might be about to confront me, but finally he smiles awkwardly, before going up to look for the bed-sheets. I'm guessing it'll take him a minute or two, because for some reason, I'm increasingly certain that this was never Clyde's house to begin with. I don't think he even knew that there was a truck in the garage, and I don't think he just *happened* to get caught by us the other day. For some reason, he seems to have wanted to get into this situation. I guess it's possible that I've become crazy and paranoid, but I can't shake the feeling that he's plotting something. He's definitely not what he seems, and I need to get away from him as fast as possible.

"Okay, Joe," I say, making sure to speak clearly so that Clyde will be able to hear me from upstairs. "I'm just gonna move you out of this draft". Grabbing the side of the table, I start dragging it across the kitchen, with Joe still on top. I'm careful not to nudge the sides, since I feel as if even the slightest bump could cause Joe's wound to re-open, but I have to get him through to the next room. What I need most of all is to get him the hell away from this place.

"Is that better?" I say, once I've got Joe through to the front-room. I hurry over to the door that leads to the garage, and then I go through and open the back of the truck. So far, everything's going according to plan. I quickly make a bed of towels, and then I head back to Joe. This is gonna be the difficult part. Carrying Joe to the truck would be difficult at the best of times, since I'm not exactly the strongest guy around; there's also the matter of the wound on his side, which looks as if it could start bleeding again at any moment. Finally, telling myself that I can't delay another second, I put my arms under Joe and pick him up. He's heavier than I expected, but I have no choice.

"Sorry," I whisper, as I struggle to carry him through the door and into the garage. To my relief, however, I'm able to quickly get him onto the back of the truck, and his wound seems to remain stable. The dried blood remains in place, and nothing else seems to be oozing out. Not yet, anyway. "We're out of here," I whisper, even though I'm not sure whether he can hear me. "I'm just gonna grab a couple of bottles of water from the kitchen". Hurrying to the front of the truck, I grab the key from my pocket and unlock the driver's side door. A sense of relief floods over me as I realize that I've got the right keys. I glance at the ignition; I know Clyde said that the truck doesn't work, but I don't believe him. I think the truck was news to him, and

I need to get a move on before he comes back downstairs. He already seems a little suspicious of me, and I can't keep coming up with excuses to get him out of the way.

Hurrying back to the kitchen, I grab a couple of bottles of water. It's crazy to think that I'm going to just abandon all the supplies on the truck, but I can't risk going out the front door. These two bottles are going to have to be enough, at least until we can find somewhere to re-stock. Suddenly it strikes me that even if Clyde's truck is working, I have no idea whether there's any gas in the tank; I guess I just have to hope for the best. I can't have everything planned out in advance. Just as I'm about to head back to the garage, I hear Clyde coming downstairs. I have time to pull the door to the front-room shut, before Clyde reappears carrying a pile of bed-sheets.

"Here," he says, clearly suspicious of my actions. "Sorry it took me a while".

"Thanks," I say. "Put them on the side. I'll set him up in a minute".

"You managed to move your brother, then?"

I nod.

"How's he doing?"

"The same," I say. "I shut the door 'cause of the cold. I figure he needs to stay warm".

"I figure you're right," he replies, staring at me. "I still think he's hurt too bad, though. I don't think he can last much longer. You need to focus on making sure he's not in pain". He pauses, and finally something seems to change; it's as if the mask has slipped a little, and he's looking at me with different eyes. "I'm not fooling you at all, am I?" he says suddenly.

I take a deep breath, as I try to work out whether I can make it through to the truck, get the key in the ignition, start her up, and pull away without Clyde catching me. Then again, I didn't think to unlock the garage door in time. It's a large wooden door, so I figure I can probably just drive straight through it, provided I can build up enough speed in the tight confines of the garage.

"You're thinking," Clyde says, with a smile. "Let me guess. You're wondering if you can get your brother through to that other truck before I manage to stop you. I'll save you the bother. You can't".

I pause. He doesn't realize I've already moved Joe to the truck, so at least I have a small advantage.

"How long have you known?" he asks.

"Known what?" I reply.

"You didn't think I just went away, did you?" he continues. "Or did you? Are you so naive, you thought I just stopped trying to get inside?" He smiles. "I stopped trying to get inside, dummy, because I was already here".

Hearing a sound over by the window, I realize the creatures outside have started trying to get inside again. Worse, I can tell from the look on his face that he's not Clyde; not really.

"I told you it was futile to run," he says. "I'm all around. I'm everywhere. I'm standing here, and I'm outside. All of me. So, really, there's only one thing left for you to do. Trust me, it won't hurt too much".

ELIZABETH

Manhattan

"HENRY!" I SHOUT, dropping to my knees as I see dark red blood pouring from the wound almost dead-center in his upper chest. Panicking, I pull off my shirt and try to stem the bleeding, but it's no use. Whatever I do, blood is still flowing from the wound, and Henry looks up at me with wide, lost eyes. He opens his mouth, as if he's going to say something, but all that comes out is a trickle of blood.

"Touching," Bob says, stepping closer and aiming the gun at me. "It's a shame this had to happen, but at least I uncovered his disloyalty before it was too late. Imagine if the situation had been more perilous and he'd caused greater problems. Don't worry, Elizabeth. You two'll be together again real soon".

Realizing it's now or never, and feeling almost as if I'm frozen in a state of shock, I lunge at Bob, pushing him to one side as he pulls the trigger. I hear the gunshot echo across the room, but to my relief I realize he didn't manage to get me. Racing through the doorway, I emerge in the yard and make my way quickly to the back of the building, hurrying through the rear offices and into the foyer. The front door is locked, of course, and I suddenly realize that there's no way out. Turning, I can already hear Bob coming after me, so I run to the stairwell. Heading up to the next floor, I decide my only chance is to get back to my parents' apartment, find the BB-gun Henry was given for his birthday a few years ago, and hope it's powerful enough to take Bob down. Once I've done that, there might still be time to save Henry.

"Where the fuck do you think you're going?" Bob shouts up at me. "You can't go anywhere! You're just trapping yourself!"

I keep going, confident that I can outrun him. Bob's a lot of things, but I doubt he's the fittest guy around.

"Let's just get this over with!" he calls up to me. "Do you really want to be out of breath when you die?"

As soon as I reach the top floor, I make my

way along to the apartment. The door turns out to be locked, but I figure I've got no choice. Stepping back, I pause for a moment before trying to kick the door down. At first, it seems hopeless; after a couple of tries, however, the locks breaks off and the door flies open, and I run inside and head straight to Henry's room.

"Come on," I mutter as I hurry to his wardrobe, desperately pulling out every box and every container in a bid to find the damn thing. I always hated the fact that it was in the apartment, and I don't even know if I can use it properly if I find it, but right now it's the only thing I can possibly think to get. Every second I waste is another second that Henry's bleeding, and another second that he's slipping closer to death. All I can think about is that I have to somehow get rid of Bob, and then I have to work out what I can do to save my brother.

"Shit!" I say, as I realize there's no sign of the BB-gun anywhere. After a moment, I realize it might be in one of the cabinets in the front room, so I hurry back along the corridor. Just as I'm next to the door, however, Bob comes lumbering through and grabs my arm, spinning me around before pushing me down to the floor.

"I was gonna kill you quick," he says, kicking me hard in the side of the chest as I try to get up. "But then you made me run up those fucking stairs, so I guess I'll take a little longer". He kicks me again, sending me sprawling across the floor. He towers over me, with a big grin on his face as if he thinks that somehow he's won. "You probably thought I couldn't catch up to you. What are you doing in here, anyway? What the fuck could you possibly use to stop me?"

"Fuck you," I mutter, trying once again to get to my feet. Before I can get far, Bob slams his knee into the side of my head, sending my thudding back down to the floor.

"Someone should have taught you some manners," he says, standing over me with the gun aimed straight at my head. "You meet a guy with a gun, you oughta be a little nicer, in case he takes badly to your foul language and decides to teach you a lesson. Didn't your parents ever take some time to show you how to treat your elders? Didn't they ever tell you to listen to other people from time to time?"

I stare up at him, filled with anger but unable to strike out at him. I know for certain that he won't hesitate to pull the trigger, but I'm running out of options.

"I *was* hoping we could all be friends," he continues, "but I guess I was naive. My first attempt to form a little group has failed, but I'll learn from my mistakes. There'll be others coming along, and I'll get it right the second time. Of course, this little meltdown wasn't entirely my fault. You and your brother have been uniquely ungrateful, despite my attempts to help, and I guess I just expected a little better. I could tell Henry was trouble, but I thought I could knock him into shape. That's always been my trouble, really. I'm just too forgiving of other peoples' faults".

"If he's dead -" I start to say.

"Who? Henry?" He smiles. "Yeah, he's dead. I'm a good shot, see? Got him right in the chest, right in the fucking heart. I don't need no second chance with a gun. Besides, these bullets are special. I had to go out of state to get 'em, and they're not entirely proper, if you know what I mean. Had to keep 'em out of sight. They splinter on impact, see, causing maximum damage. Military-level issue". He pauses for a moment. "I'm just sorry we never managed to get a bit closer, Elizabeth. I truly believed I'd be able to bring you round to my way of thinking. I was looking forward to getting down to business and starting a new generation. I know you were probably dreading the thought, but I think you'd have come around eventually. I can be quite a sensual lover. Then again, I guess once you're dead, I can have a little practice, huh?" He laughs at his own joke. "Well, I figure, why not? You'll stay warm for a few hours".

"Go to hell," I say, getting ready to lunge for the gun. It's a long shot, but it's all I can think to do.

"You're just a coward," I add after a moment.

"I don't feel much like a coward right now," he replies. "I feel like I'm doing pretty damn good".

"Well, you -" I suddenly remember the hunting knife wedged into my belt. It's not much, and it's still a long shot, but if I can get close enough, I might be able to get at him before he has a chance to pull the trigger. "Why don't you show me what you can do?" I ask, hoping to maybe distract him by trying to seduce him. "You keep talking about getting me pregnant, but I don't see any sign of you making a move. What's wrong? Scared?"

He smiles. "Think I'm that dumb, do you? Think I'm that easily distracted?"

"Maybe," I reply, fixing him with a determined stare. "Or maybe you're just scared". Biting my bottom lip, I can see that I've managed to get Bob's attention. For a moment, he seems to be wavering, as if I might actually have started to bring him around to the idea.

"Slut," he says suddenly.

"You don't like sluts?" I ask, slowly reaching down toward the knife in my belt. "Aren't sluts your kind of thing, Bob?"

"Sluts are only good for one thing," he says.

"And what's that?"

He smiles. "You won't reach that fucking knife".

I freeze.

"Nice try," he says, before kicking me so hard in the side of the face, I'm send sprawling across the floor. "Very, very nice try. Most men would've fallen for that and ended up with a knife in their gut, but I'm afraid you picked the wrong guy to mess with, Elizabeth. I'm not so easily led".

"Fucking coward," I mutter, spitting blood out onto the floor.

"What did you call me?" he shouts.

"You -" Before I can say anything else, Bob grabs me by the waist and hauls me up onto my feet. Holding my arms tight behind my back, he tosses his gun onto the sofa and pushes me over to the broken window. A cold wind is blowing into the apartment as Bob gets me right up against the sill.

"You think I'm a coward?" he sneers, spitting into my ear. "You think that, just 'cause I didn't pull your panties down the first time I met you? You think I didn't want to?" He leans closer, sniffing my neck like a pig. "You think I didn't recognize you for a slut and a whore? I could tell what you were, the first time I every laid eyes on you. Running in and out of the building with your friends. Well, I'm sorry, Elizabeth Marter, but I'm afraid I'm a gentleman, and I decided to try and treat you right, to give you a chance to be less of a fucking bitch. Obviously, that turned out to not be such a good idea, but at least I can hold my head up high".

He presses me down onto the broken glass, which cuts a line across my chest. I let out a gasp of pain as the shards dig deep into my flesh, but I'm determined not to scream. Looking down, I see the sidewalk far, far below.

"Or do you think I'm a coward because I use a gun?" he continues. "Is that what bothers you? Well, fuck that, I don't need a gun to dispose of a slutty whore like you. You think a guy like me needs to hide behind some little piece of metal? I was gonna keep you alive so I could fuck you a few times, but I guess that's out of the question now. I wouldn't touch you if you were the last woman on the fucking planet. I need someone who can offer some decent genes to our kids, not a putrid little whore". He pauses for a moment. "I'm very sorry, Elizabeth, but this is gonna have to be goodbye. There's no way back from what you did. I hope you have time on the way down to repent for your disloyalty".

"Fuck -" I start to say, but suddenly Bob grabs me by the waist and pushes me out through the window. Twisting, I reach out and grab the edge of the window just in time. My hand digs into the broken glass, but I can't let go; the rest of my body is dangling out the window, hundreds of meters up above the sidewalk.

"Still clinging on, huh?" Bob says, smiling

down at me. "What are you gonna do? Promise to fuck me if I pull you up?"

I try to get some kind of grip with my feet, but the side of the building is too smooth. Scrabbling desperately for some kind of hold, I look up at Bob and see the grin on his face. He thinks he's won. He thinks he's got everything he wanted, and he thinks there's nothing I can do to get back up.

"You're gonna scream as you fall," he says, placing his hands on mine and slowly starting to pull them loose from the edge of the window. "Who's a coward now, huh?"

Pulling one of my hands away, I reach down to my belt and feel the hilt of the knife. Realizing it's now or never, I pull the knife loose and then I use my other arm to haul myself up, even though this means gripping the broken window frame so hard, the glass digs deep into my hand. Before Bob can react, I plunge the knife straight into the center of his chest, feeling the blade scraping against his ribs before it slips between and lodges itself firmly in his body. Letting go of the window ledge with my other hand, I reach up until finally I'm hanging from the knife as it lodges in Bob's chest. If it slips out of his body, I'll fall.

"You fucking -" he starts to say, with blood starting to pour from his mouth.

With my very last ounce of energy, I haul

myself up. The knife is between Bob's ribs, but I can feel it starting to bend a little. Finally, I scramble back through the window, pushing Bob back into the room in the process. He takes a few steps away, before turning and looking over at the gun.

"No way," I say, hurrying to the sofa, grabbing the gun, and turning to him. I hold the gun up, aiming straight at Bob's face. For a moment, I feel as if I can't do this; I can't actually kill him. After a second, however, I'm overcome by a sudden feeling of strength: I *can* do this. After all, Bob shot my brother, so why can't I do the same thing to him? I've always hated guns, and I've always seen them as a weapon used by cowards. Right now, however, I've come to realize that I was wrong; sometimes, a gun's really all you need.

"You..." He grabs the hilt of the knife and slowly slides it out from his chest. Blood pours from the wound, and it's clear that he's getting weaker by the second. "You fucking little bitch," he blurts out, his mouth filling with blood.

"Yeah," I say, taking a deep breath to steady my nerves. "Well, so what?" With that, I pull the trigger and shoot Bob straight in the center of his face. His forehead explodes and he falls backward, crashing into the cabinets before finally slumping down to the ground. His body twitches for a moment, but finally he falls still. Just to be absolutely certain that he's gone, I step forward, place the gun against his temple, and fire one more time. The other side of his head is blasted apart, with bits of bone and brain slopping down onto the ground.

"Fuck you, asshole," I whisper.

I take a step back, as an icy wind blows through the apartment. It's almost as if I can still hear the gunshot echoing through my mind. After a moment, I turn and look over at the door. "Henry!" I shout, before racing out of the room.

THOMAS

Oklahoma

"I WAS HOPING TO last a little longer," Clyde says as he steps closer. "That was the idea, anyway. I mean, controlling the other bodies is easy, but I wanted to see if I could control one that was freshly dead, and make it so that no-one could tell the difference. I think I did a pretty good job, all in all, but obviously I should have done some research in advance. Still, I fooled you, didn't I? You couldn't tell it was me".

Taking a step back, I try to work out what to do. If I can just find some way to delay Clyde, I have a chance of getting to the truck, but I don't think it's going to be the work of a moment to slow him down. Besides, he's going to have reinforcements soon: the other creatures are clawing at the window and trying to push the door open.

"I should have prepared better," he continues. "I know that, but I just wanted to see how I'd do. I mean, it was easy enough, piloting those rotting dead bodies around. But I wanted to do more. I wanted to see if I could make one seem like it was still alive". He pauses for a moment, and he un-tucks his shirt and lifts it up to reveal that his belly is slightly distended, with the skin turning a familiar gray tone. "This body has barely rotted. Just a few bits here and there so far. It seemed like the perfect opportunity to - Hang on". He frowns. "I don't speak a fucking word!" he says firmly, before smiling again. "Sorry, I'm controlling another body in Beijing right now. This guy's babbling at me in Chinese, begging me not to kill him". He blinks a couple of times. "There. Done. Sorry, I'm still getting used to piloting multiple bodies at the same time".

"When did you change?" I ask. My heart's racing as I back slowly toward the other side of the kitchen. There's a knife on the counter, which I figure is better than nothing.

"Change?" He walks over to the front door and slides the lock across, allowing the door to swing open. Several of the creatures start to enter the room. "I didn't really change, not while you were around. This was just one of the many bodies at my disposal, but fortunately this one wasn't too badly bloated. I thought it'd be fun to see if I could trick you, and I did pretty well. But the time for stupid games is over".

Grabbing the knife, I hold it out toward him.

"You think that's gonna be much use?" he asks, laughing. "You really don't understand the severity of your situation, do you? There are *billions* of me. You kill this body, there's a dozen more right outside, and more all over the world. That's the whole point of the virus; it's a way for me to spread and control almost every body on the planet. I'm everyone, and I'm all around. I'm coming through the front door, the back door, the windows. I'm not gonna stop coming for you, Thomas. All of you. Every survivor".

"Who are you?" I ask, playing for time while I come up with a plan. I figure I could get through to the next room and push some furniture against the door. Clyde thinks I still need to move Joe's body, so I've got a small advantage, but not much.

"My name was Joseph," he says, as the other creatures continue to crowd into the room. "Joseph Drachman. Remember that name. It's the name of the man who changed the world. It's the name of the man who used his DNA to clone a virus in his own image. I turned myself into a virus and now I'm everywhere, connected all around the world. Not just infecting bodies, but I'm literally everywhere.

I'm on the floor, I'm on the walls. Bacterial life has always been the dominant life-form on this planet. To humans, this whole thing might seem like a mass extinction event, but I don't give a shit about humans. This is about me, bridging the divide between humanity and bacteria, and becoming both. This isn't a mass extinction event, it's a mass life event, and I'm the life".

Realizing that he seems to be getting distracted by his own speech, I decide it's time to make a break for the garage. I still don't quite understand what Clyde means, but I can tell he's struggling to remain focused. It's as if his concentration is wandering, and he keeps getting distracted by something I can't see. Any second now, I'm going to run. The other creatures are staring at me, and they seem to have fallen still, as if Clyde's too caught up in himself to notice what's happening.

"Sorry," Clyde says eventually. "I'm having a conversation with some guy in Germany. I don't... You don't speak German, do you?"

"Me?"

He nods.

"No".

"Damn it," he continues. "I thought I'd planned ahead. I thought I'd prepared for every eventuality, but I forgot that there'd be a language issue. Hang on, let me just break his neck". He pauses, and finally he smiles. "There. Done".

"You're crazy," I say.

"Of course," he replies. "My growth over the past week has been exponential. No-one could go through this without losing their mind a little, at least temporarily. In a way, it's good that there are still some survivors to be killed. It gives me focus. A few of you turned out to have natural immunity, but that's only to be expected. I'll have fun mopping up the stragglers, and finally I'll be the only one here. The whole planet, just me. Perfection, really. I've got to admit, it was a crazy idea, and I wasn't at all sure it'd work. But here I am, inhabiting all these dead bodies. It's taking a little time to learn how to control so *many* bodies all at once. I guess each mind was supposed to control one body, and now look at me, controlling billions. But I'm getting there. Don't worry about that. Seeing the world from so many different vantage points, that's not something you can get used to very quickly. Right now, for example, I'm seeing the view from all over the world, all at once. Honestly, it's enough to drive someone crazy. The human mind isn't designed to cope with such an influx, but I'm learning to deal with it slowly. I'll get there eventually, but for now, I'm sorry if I seem a little crazy or a little scattered. I really must apologize for the slightly distracted manner in which I'm about to kill you -"

And that's when I do it. I turn and run.

Heading through to the next room, I slam the door shut and push a small table across the entrance. It's not going to hold him, though, and I look around for something else to use.

"Seriously?" Clyde calls out from the kitchen. "You think you can escape? I'm everywhere!"

At that moment, a nearby window smashes. Two more creatures start climbing through, and one of them grins as it looks over at me. "See?" the creature says, "you're really not gonna be able to -" He looks across the room, and for a moment he seems surprised. "You already got him on the truck?" he asks. "Clever boy. When did you do that?"

Not waiting to give him an answer, I turn and hurry through to the garage. Getting into the driver's seat, I slip the key into the ignition and find, to my relief, that the engine starts beautifully, first time. I pull the door shut and stare ahead at the garage door. The wheels spin for a moment before the truck shoots forward, smashing straight through the door and then lumbering down the driveway and out into the street. Looking back, I feel a moment's relief that Clyde doesn't seem to be following us, but then I look forward and see two of the creatures coming straight toward the truck.

Without a second thought, I turn the wheel and drive away, knocking one of the creatures down in the process. I feel a heavy bump as the wheels run straight over the creature, but I don't have time to even register what just happened: all I can think about is the fact that I have to get out of here as fast as possible, and that I have to get far, far away from Scottsville. Glancing over my shoulder, I see Joe's motionless body in the back of the truck. I want to stop and check that he's okay, but I can't risk being caught by Clyde or any of the other creatures.

"Joe!" I shout. "Are you okay back there?"

The truck bounces over a bump in the road, and I see Joe's body jolting around. I don't know whether he's still alive, but I can't afford to stop and check just yet.

As the truck speeds past the last building of Scottsville and I head out into the countryside, I realize that I've actually made it. I look at the rear-view mirror as Scottsville recedes into the distance. Whatever else happens, I have to keep away from towns from now on; they're too dangerous, and people like Clyde could be waiting around every corner. I just have to keep going and hope I can find some way to help Joe, otherwise I'll be completely alone out here. Even though I'm now well clear of the town, I tell myself that it's too early to relax just yet. I need to keep going, which means there's no time to stop and check on Joe. I guess, in a way, I'm delaying the moment where I check to see if he's still alive. But he has to be. He's my brother. He's

Joe. He's the toughest bastard I ever met in my life, and he's not gonna let some gash in his chest be the end of him. I can trust him to stay alive on the back of the truck, just as he can trust me to get us to safety.

ELIZABETH

Manhattan

WHEN I FIND HENRY, I can see immediately that it's too late. He's still on the floor, in the middle of a pool of blood, and he's not moving. Pausing in the doorway, frozen in place, I feel my mind empty of all thoughts; I'm just here, cold and alone, staring at my brother's dead body.

"Henry?" I say eventually, not because I think there's any chance of him being alive, but because I feel like I have to at least try.

No answer.

The room feels so still and quiet, like a grave.

I want to turn and run, to get as far from here as possible, but I know I have to stay. I have to at least check to see if he's alive, for my own sake. Stepping into the room and walking around the puddle of blood, I look down at his face. He's so pale, probably due to all the blood he's lost, and his eyes are open, staring down at the floor. One of his arms is reaching out beyond the puddle, the hand open as if he was reaching for something when he died.

I walk around and kneel next to the hand, and finally I reach down and take it in mine. His skin's so cold, it's hard to believe it's real; it feels more like I'm holding the hand of some kind of waxwork. Sitting in stunned silence, feeling as if there's some kind of damn building up in my chest, preventing me from crying, I feel as if the whole world has stopped for a moment.

Suddenly I feel something. The slightest pressure from his hand, as if he's squeezing my fingers to let me know he's alive. I lean closer, and finally I notice a flicker in his eyes.

"Henry?" I say, shifting toward him, my knees soaking in the puddle of blood. "Henry, can you hear me?"

His eyes open for a moment, just slightly.

"Henry," I continue, "it's going to be okay, I..." I stare at him, and I realize it's not going to be okay at all. Reaching over, I put a finger against his neck to check his pulse. There's a very faint beating sensation, but it's clear that he's only got a few minutes to live. Not knowing what else to do, I lean down and kiss his cold forehead. "I love you," I say, squeezing his hand tight.

We sit like this for several minutes, and finally I force myself to check his pulse again. This time, there's nothing. I reach down and close his eyes. All I can hope now is that somehow, by some kind of miracle, he was aware of me in those final moments.

"I'm so sorry," I whisper, kissing his forehead again. "I should have stayed. I should have found a way to..." My voice trails off, as I think back to all the chances I had to save him. Finally, tears start rolling down my cheeks as the full force of the moment hits me. My chest feels so tight and heavy, as if my whole body is going to burst, and I spend several minutes just sitting and sobbing, with my face against my brother's head.

Eventually, I look up and it hits me: I'm alone. I'm completely alone in New York, barring any sudden encounters with strangers. My family is gone, my friends are gone, and Mallory's group could be anywhere by now. Sitting back, with my knees soaked in Henry's blood, I try to work out what to do but, instead, my mind goes completely blank. It's as if I'm stranded and unable to move, and everything around me has stopped.

I have to get out of here.

I've never been so clear about anything in my

life: I have to get out of New York. I have to go after Mallory, I have to leave this place behind, I have to -

Suddenly there's a huge boom in the distance, and the entire building starts to shake. Plaster comes crashing down from the ceiling, but the boom ends and the building comes to a rest. My heart's racing. I don't know what that was, but it seemed like it was very, very far away and very, very big.

THOMAS

Oklahoma

AS THE TRUCK RACES along the dusty, deserted road, there's a sudden boom in the distance. Everything starts to shake: the horizon, the road, everything. I struggle for a moment to bring the truck under control, and finally the back-end flicks out, sending us skidding sideways to a halt as the shaking stops.

"What the hell was that?" I say out loud, glancing back at Joe.

No answer. He's barely conscious.

"Joe?"

I pause. I know I should go and check on him, but... It still might not be safe. I'll wait a little longer.

"Hey there," says a voice nearby.

Turning, I see a guy standing next to the truck. He's pretty weird-looking, and kind of scruffy. Although he doesn't *look* sick, I immediately tense up, fearing the worst.

"Where'd you come from?" I ask, reaching down to make sure the door's locked.

"I'm just making my way somewhere new," he says with a smile.

I glance over my shoulder, in case there's anyone else around. I swear I didn't spot this guy, not until the truck stopped.

"Who's the guy in the back?" the man asks. "Is seems hurt".

"I'm taking him to get help," I say.

"Then I shouldn't hold you back any longer," the man says, reaching into his pocket and pulling out a large white feather. "This is for you".

I stare at him. The guy might not be sick, but I'm starting to think he's a bit strange in the head.

"Don't you want it?" he asks, frowning.

"Just leave it on the truck," I say cautiously.

Smiling, the guy places the white feather in the back of the truck, next to Joe.

"I'm not giving you a ride," I stammer. "There's no way -"

"I don't want a ride," he says, stepping back. "I'd rather walk". He pauses for a moment. " Shouldn't you get going? Your brother needs help".

Feeling kind of bad for leaving the guy by the side of the road, I put the truck back in gear and get us going again. I have no idea what caused that boom and the shaking, but right now I really don't want to stick around and find out. I glance in the rear-view mirror, but the guy already seems to have disappeared. Whoever he was, I don't need to get distracted right now. I just need to focus on the road ahead, and pray that there's a miracle around the next corner.

EPILOGUE

Two weeks ago

"YOU WANT ANOTHER ONE?"

Looking up from his empty glass, Joseph finds himself face to face with the bartender.

"Uh... Yeah, sure," he replies. "Same again, or something similar. Whatever".

Seemingly unimpressed, the bartender grabs the glass and heads over to fill it with another whiskey.

Looking at his watch, Joseph does a few mental calculations and realizes that it's almost time. He's waited so long, and now the moment is about to arrive. It might be in a second, or a minute, or even an hour, but it's coming. It's coming today. The moment when all his plans come to fruition and the world finally learns what's coming; the moment when everyone dies.

"You want me to add that to your tab?" the bartender asks, bringing the drink back over.

"Yes, please," Joseph says, smiling. "Add it to my tab".

"Tab's getting pretty long," the barman grunts.

Joseph reaches into his pocket and pulls out a wad of notes, which he places in front of the barman with a satisfied smirk. "Take whatever I owe you. Add a tip, whatever you think's fair to compensate you for your extraordinary service".

Raising his eyebrows, the barman reaches out to take some cash, before pausing to clear his throat.

"Nasty cough you've got there," Joseph says. "Had it long?"

"Just came today," the barman replies, counting out his money. "Knowing my luck, I'm coming down with something. Don't worry, though. I'm washin' my hands plenty. You won't get nothing from me".

"I'm not worried," Joseph says, grinning as the barman heads over to the register.

Picking up his glass, Joseph pauses for a moment before taking a gulp of whiskey. He watches as the barman goes to grab some empty glasses from the other side of the room. Such a bland, dull little scene, and one that Joseph wouldn't normally notice; today, however, even the tiniest and most mundane of activities seems to carry a little extra poignancy, since everything is soon going to end. This barman, for example, will probably soon clean his last table, and serve his last drink.

"I'm closing in ten," the barman calls back to him.

"That's fine," Joseph says, finishing his drink and getting up from the stool. "I was thinking of heading home, anyway". He grabs the rest of his money and heads over to the door, pausing for a moment to glance back and watch as the barman suffers a brief coughing fit. "Get well soon," he says quietly, unable to stop smiling as he heads out into the cold night air.

DAYS 5 TO 8

Continued in:

Days 9 to 16
(Mass Extinction Event book 3)

Also by Amy Cross

The Devil, the Witch and the Whore
(The Deal book 1)

"Leave the forest alone. Whatever's out there, just let it be. Don't make it angry."

When a horrific discovery is made at the edge of town, Sheriff James Kopperud realizes the answers he seeks might be waiting beyond in the vast forest. But everybody in the town of Deal knows that there's something out there in the forest, something that should never be disturbed. A deal was made long ago, a deal that was supposed to keep the town safe. And if he insists on investigating the murder of a local girl, James is going to have to break that deal and head out into the wilderness.

Meanwhile, James has no idea that his estranged daughter Ramsey has returned to town. Ramsey is running from something, and she thinks she can find safety in the vast tunnel system that runs beneath the forest. Before long, however, Ramsey finds herself coming face to face with creatures that hide in the shadows. One of these creatures is known as the devil, and another is known as the witch. They're both waiting for the whore to arrive, but for very different reasons. And soon Ramsey is offered a terrible deal, one that could save or destroy the entire town, and maybe even the world.

Also by Amy Cross

The Soul Auction

"I saw a woman on the beach. I watched her face a demon."

Thirty years after her mother's death, Alice Ashcroft is drawn back to the coastal English town of Curridge. Somebody in Curridge has been reviewing Alice's novels online, and in those reviews there have been tantalizing hints at a hidden truth. A truth that seems to be linked to her dead mother.

"Thirty years ago, there was a soul auction."

Once she reaches Curridge, Alice finds strange things happening all around her. Something attacks her car. A figure watches her on the beach at night. And when she tries to find the person who has been reviewing her books, she makes a horrific discovery.

What really happened to Alice's mother thirty years ago? Who was she talking to, just moments before dropping dead on the beach? What caused a huge rockfall that nearly tore a nearby cliff-face in half? And what sinister presence is lurking in the grounds of the local church?

Also by Amy Cross

Darper Danver: The Complete First Series

Five years ago, three friends went to a remote cabin in the woods and tried to contact the spirit of a long-dead soldier. They thought they could control whatever happened next. They were wrong...

Newly released from prison, Cassie Briggs returns to Fort Powell, determined to get her life back on track. Soon, however, she begins to suspect that an ancient evil still lurks in the nearby cabin. Was the mysterious Darper Danver really destroyed all those years ago, or does her spirit still linger, waiting for a chance to return?

As Cassie and her ex-boyfriend Fisher are finally forced to face the truth about what happened in the cabin, they realize that Darper isn't ready to let go of their lives just yet. Meanwhile, a vengeful woman plots revenge for her brother's murder, and a New York ghost writer arrives in town to uncover the truth. Before long, strange carvings begin to appear around town and blood starts to flow once again.

Also by Amy Cross

The Ghost of Molly Holt

"Molly Holt is dead. There's nothing to fear in this house."

When three teenagers set out to explore an abandoned house in the middle of a forest, they think they've found the location where the infamous Molly Holt video was filmed.

They've found much more than that...

Tim doesn't believe in ghosts, but he has a crush on a girl who does. That's why he ends up taking her out to the house, and it's also why he lets her take his only flashlight. But as they explore the house together, Tim and Becky start to realize that something else might be lurking in the shadows.

Something that, ten years ago, suffered unimaginable pain.

Something that won't rest until a terrible wrong has been put right.

Also by Amy Cross

American Coven

He kidnapped three women and held them in his basement. He thought they couldn't fight back. He was wrong...

Snatched from the street near her home, Holly Carter is taken to a rural house and thrown down into a stone basement. She meets two other women who have also been kidnapped, and soon Holly learns about the horrific rituals that take place in the house. Eventually, she's called upstairs to take her place in the ice bath.

As her nightmare continues, however, Holly learns about a mysterious power that exists in the basement, and which the three women might be able to harness. When they finally manage to get through the metal door, however, the women have no idea that their fight for freedom is going to stretch out for more than a decade, or that it will culminate in a final, devastating demonstration of their new-found powers.

Also by Amy Cross

The Ash House

Why would anyone ever return to a haunted house?

For Diane Mercer the answer is simple. She's dying of cancer, and she wants to know once and for all whether ghosts are real.

Heading home with her young son, Diane is determined to find out whether the stories are real. After all, everyone else claimed to see and hear strange things in the house over the years. Everyone except Diane had some kind of experience in the house, or in the little ash house in the yard.

As Diane explores the house where she grew up, however, her son is exploring the yard and the forest. And while his mother might be struggling to come to terms with her own impending death, Daniel Mercer is puzzled by fleeting appearances of a strange little girl who seems drawn to the ash house, and by strange, rasping coughs that he keeps hearing at night.

The Ash House is a horror novel about a woman who desperately wants to know what will happen to her when she dies, and about a boy who uncovers the shocking truth about a young girl's murder.

Also by Amy Cross

Haunted

Twenty years ago, the ghost of a dead little girl drove
Sheriff Michael Blaine to his death.

Now, that same ghost is coming for his daughter.

Returning to the small town where she grew up, Alex
Roberts is determined to live a normal, quiet life. For the
residents of Railham, however, she's an unwelcome
reminder of the town's darkest hour.

Twenty years ago, nine-year-old Mo Garvey was found
brutally murdered in a nearby forest. Everyone thinks
that Alex's father was responsible, but if the killer was
brought to justice, why is the ghost of Mo Garvey still
after revenge?

And how far will the real killer go to protect his secret,
when Alex starts getting closer to the truth?

Haunted is a horror novel about a woman who has to
face her past, about a town that would rather forget, and
about a little girl who refuses to let death stand in her
way.

Also by Amy Cross

The Curse of Wetherley House

"If you walk through that door, Evil Mary will get you."

When she agrees to visit a supposedly haunted house with an old friend, Rosie assumes she'll encounter nothing more scary than a few creaks and bumps in the night. Even the legend of Evil Mary doesn't put her off. After all, she knows ghosts aren't real. But when Mary makes her first appearance, Rosie realizes she might already be trapped.

For more than a century, Wetherley House has been cursed. A horrific encounter on a remote road in the late 1800's has already caused a chain of misery and pain for all those who live at the house. Wetherley House was abandoned long ago, after a terrible discovery in the basement, something has remained undetected within its room. And even the local children know that Evil Mary waits in the house for anyone foolish enough to walk through the front door.

Before long, Rosie realizes that her entire life has been defined by the spirit of a woman who died in agony. Can she become the first person to escape Evil Mary, or will she fall victim to the same fate as the house's other occupants?

Also by Amy Cross

The Ghosts of Hexley Airport

Ten years ago, more than two hundred people died in a horrific plane crash at Hexley Airport.

Today, some say their ghosts still haunt the terminal building.

When she starts her new job at the airport, working a night shift as part of the security team, Casey assumes the stories about the place can't be true. Even when she has a strange encounter in a deserted part of the departure hall, she's certain that ghosts aren't real.

Soon, however, she's forced to face the truth. Not only is there something haunting the airport's buildings and tarmac, but a sinister force is working behind the scenes to replicate the circumstances of the original accident. And as a snowstorm moves in, Hexley Airport looks set to witness yet another disaster.

Also by Amy Cross

The Girl Who Never Came Back

Twenty years ago, Charlotte Abernathy vanished while playing near her family's house. Despite a frantic search, no trace of her was found until a year later, when the little girl turned up on the doorstep with no memory of where she'd been.

Today, Charlotte has put her mysterious ordeal behind her, even though she's never learned where she was during that missing year. However, when her eight-year-old niece vanishes in similar circumstances, a fully-grown Charlotte is forced to make a fresh attempt to uncover the truth.

Originally published in 2013, the fully revised and updated version of *The Girl Who Never Came Back* tells the harrowing story of a woman who thought she could forget her past, and of a little girl caught in the tangled web of a dark family secret.

Also by Amy Cross

Asylum
(The Asylum Trilogy book 1)

"No-one ever leaves Lakehurst. The staff, the patients, the ghosts... Once you're here, you're stuck forever."

After shooting her little brother dead, Annie Radford is sent to Lakehurst psychiatric hospital for assessment. Hearing voices in her head, Annie is forced to undergo experimental new treatments devised by a mysterious old man who lives in the hospital's attic. It soon becomes clear that the hospital's staff, led by the vicious Nurse Winter, are hiding something horrific at Lakehurst.

As Annie struggles to survive the hospital, she learns more about Nurse Winter's own story. Once a promising young medical student, Kirsten Winter also heard voices in her head. Voices that traveled a long way to reach her. Voices that have a plan of their own. Voices that will stop at nothing to get what they want.

What kind of signals are being transmitted from the basement of the hospital? Who is the old man in the attic? Why are living human brains kept in jars? And what is the dark secret that lurks at the heart of the hospital?

Also by Amy Cross

The Devil's Hand

"I felt it last night! I was all alone, and suddenly a hand touched my shoulder!"

The year is 1943. Beacon's Ash is a private, remote school in the North of England, and all its pupils are fallen girls. Pregnant and unmarried, they have been sent away by their families. For Ivy Jones, a young girl who arrived at the school several months earlier, Beacon's Ash is a nightmare, and her fears are strengthened when one of her classmates is killed in mysterious circumstances.

Has the ghost of Abigail Cartwright returned to the school? Who or what is responsible for the hand that touches the girls' shoulders in the dead of night? And is the school's headmaster Jeremiah Kane just a madman who seeks to cause misery, or is he in fact on the trail of the Devil himself? Soon ghosts are stalking the dark corridors, and Ivy realizes she has to face the evil that lurks in the school's shadows.

The Devil's Hand is a horror novel about a girl who seeks the truth about her friend's death, and about a madman who believes the Devil stalks the school's corridors in the run-up to Christmas.

For more information, visit:

www. amycross.com

AMY CROSS

Made in the USA
Middletown, DE
06 October 2021

49772590R00187